The kiss and all it meant, all that it made her want, shook Anna.

"Don't," she cried.

"Don't what?" he demanded. "Don't kiss you? Don't want you? The kissing I can control if I have to. The wanting I can't. I don't want to stop wanting you. Don't tell me you don't feel the same, because we both know you'd be lying, and you're a lousy liar, Anna."

"It doesn't matter what either of us feels."

"The hell it doesn't. It's the *only* thing that matters."

"It doesn't matter," she repeated, her heart breaking. "Gavin, you leaving. So what's the point?"

She was right. But the emotion in her voice, the pain he heard, twisted in his chest.

"Yes, I'll have to leave soon. But is that supposed to mean that we just turn our backs on whatever this is that's happening between us and pretend it doesn't exist?"

Dear Reader,

During this holiday season, don't forget to treat *yourself* special, too. And taking the time to enjoy November's Special Edition lineup is the perfect place to start!

Veteran author Lisa Jackson continues her FOREVER FAMILY miniseries with *A Family Kind of Gal*. All THAT SPECIAL WOMAN! Tiffany Santini wants is a life of harmony away from her domineering in-laws. But there's no avoiding her sinfully sexy brother-in-law when he lavishes her—and her kids—with attention. Look for the third installment of this engaging series in January 1999.

And there's more continuing drama on the way! First, revisit the Adams family with *The Cowgirl & The Unexpected Wedding* when Sherryl Woods delivers book four in the popular AND BABY MAKES THREE: THE NEXT GENERATION series. Next, the PRESCRIPTION: MARRIAGE medical series returns with *Prince Charming, M.D.* by Susan Mallery. Just about every nurse at Honeygrove Memorial Hospital has been swooning over one debonair doc—except the R.N. who recalls her old flame's track record for breaking hearts! Then the MEN OF THE DOUBLE-C RANCH had better look out when a sassy redhead gets under a certain ornery cowboy's skin in *The Rancher and the Redhead* by Allison Leigh.

Rounding off this month, Janis Reams Hudson shares a lighthearted tale about a shy accountant who discovers a sexy stranger sleeping on her sofa in *Until You*. And in *A Mother for Jeffrey* by Trisha Alexander, a heroine realizes her lifelong dream of having a family.

I hope you enjoy all of our books this month. Happy Thanksgiving from all of us at Silhouette Books.

Sincerely,

Karen Taylor Richman
Senior Editor

Please address questions and book requests to:
Silhouette Reader Service
U.S.: 3010 Walden Ave., P.O. Box 1325, Buffalo, NY 14269
Canadian: P.O. Box 609, Fort Erie, Ont. L2A 5X3

JANIS REAMS HUDSON

UNTIL YOU

Silhouette®

SPECIAL ▼ EDITION®

Published by Silhouette Books
America's Publisher of Contemporary Romance

SILHOUETTE BOOKS

ISBN 0-373-24210-7

UNTIL YOU

Books by Janis Reams Hudson

Silhouette Special Edition

Resist Me if You Can #1037
The Mother of His Son #1095
His Daughter's Laughter #1105
Until You #1210

JANIS REAMS HUDSON

was born in California, grew up in Colorado, lived in Texas for a few years and now calls central Oklahoma home. She is the author of more than twenty novels, both contemporary and historical romances. Her books have appeared on the Waldenbooks, B. Dalton and Bookrack bestseller lists and earned numerous awards, including the National Readers' Choice Award and Reviewer's Choice awards from *Romantic Times Magazine*. She is a three-time finalist for the coveted RITA Award from Romance Writers of America and is the past president of RWA.

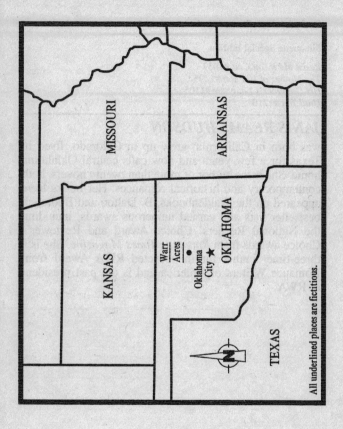

MISSOURI

ARKANSAS

KANSAS

OKLAHOMA

Warr
Acres
•
Oklahoma
City ★

TEXAS

N

All underlined places are fictitious.

Chapter One

It had been a typical, busy week at work, ending with a typical, frantic Friday. All indications pointed to a typical, restful weekend in Oklahoma City's typical, quiet suburb of Warr Acres.

Until she got home.

Anna Collins pulled into her driveway Friday evening and put the car in park. With the engine still running, she got out and walked slowly to the mailbox on her front porch. She wanted to run, but that would have been unseemly.

Be there, be there.

When she reached into the mailbox, her hand trembled. She fingered the envelopes, then carefully pulled them out. A bill from Oklahoma Gas and Electric. A coupon for ladies' day at a local muffler shop. A long brown envelope from—

It came. It came.

With a quick look around to make sure no one was watching, Anna hugged the envelope with the return address of the University of Central Oklahoma to her chest and sighed deeply. *It came.* Finally. Her admission form.

All she had to do now was fill it out, mail it in with her high school transcript and college entrance exam test scores, then wait to hear if she'd been admitted. There should be no problem there. Then she would enroll and start classes.

Finally. Anna Lee Collins was going to college.

Since childhood she had dreamed of going to college. Dreaming wasn't something Anna Collins normally allowed herself, but this one had been virtually impossible to squelch. It had also been nearly impossible to achieve. She was thirty years old, and just now applying for admission. It had taken her that long to pay off her parents' debts, straighten out her life, her brother's life, her own finances.

But she had the money now. It was finally going to happen. Even though she would have to keep working during the day and attend classes at night, she couldn't be happier. The accounting degree she coveted was within her grasp.

College! I'm going to college!

Still clutching the envelope tightly in one hand, Anna whirled and took two skipping hops before recovering her sense of decorum and walking sedately back to the driveway. She pulled a key from her pocket and unlocked the garage door. After all these years, raising the door shouldn't be so difficult, but it was old, heavy and liked to stick in damp weather. In Oklahoma, it was always damp. She and the door both groaned with the effort it took to raise it. Then Anna groaned again at the sight that greeted her.

Her brother's motorcycle.

"No," she said with a quiet moan of despair. Then she uttered a quick prayer for forgiveness. She loved Ben. Really she did. But…but…

But nothing. Just because he'd come home unannounced—again—didn't mean he'd come home for money. Again. Did it?

If he had come for money, what would she do? She had budgeted herself so tightly for the next few years that she knew she didn't have a penny to spare. But she had never told Ben no before. Was it fair to start now, with no warning?

Anna chewed on her bottom lip. When she caught herself, she quit. Standing in the garage worrying wasn't doing any good. She stepped back out onto the driveway and tugged the door down. With his motorcycle parked right in the middle of the one-car garage, there was no room for her eighteen-year-old Chevy.

She shut the car engine off, gathered her keys and purse, and went back to the front door, the precious envelope from U.C.O. still clutched in her hand. She entered the house quietly in case Ben was sleeping. If he'd ridden all night to get home, which was usually the case, he would be sacked out on the couch or his bed, facedown and dead to the world for maybe as long as eighteen hours. Why any sane person would deliberately choose to punish himself that way, she would never understand. He thought it was a lark to drive all night, and he loved nothing more than to sleep all day.

Sure enough, there he was, sprawled facedown on the living room couch, apparently dead to the world. He wore nothing but a pair of ratty, faded jeans, the seat of which was worn white and thin. A white T-shirt lay draped over a duffel bag sitting neatly against the wall. Beside it were a pair of brown leather boots, a small black shaving kit, a screaming yellow helmet and…a guitar? When had he started playing the guitar?

To Anna's sense of orderliness, the room was a mess. But for Ben, it was actually quite tidy. If he'd been home longer than sixty seconds his belongings were usually strewn from one end of the house to the other. The last time, he'd even had the audacity to stack a pyramid of empty beer cans on her oak-and-glass coffee table sometime during the night while she'd slept.

Oh, the tongue-lashing she'd given him, not only for that, but for having come home drunk the night before and parking his motorcycle in her flower bed.

There had been no repeat of that sort of thing, thank heaven. And now here he was, being neat—for him, at least—with his belongings. It was, by all appearances, a miracle.

She shook her head in wonder and closed the front door behind her softly so as not to wake him. No telling how far away he'd come from this time. Judging by the new lighter streaks in his dark brown hair and the golden tan on his bare back, he may have come from the beach. She just had no idea which one; East Coast, West Coast, or the Gulf. And he'd been working out, too. She didn't remember his back and arms being quite so muscular the last time he was home.

"Ben?"

Nothing. Not even a groan.

Anna shrugged. She should be used to the way he dropped into her life whenever the mood struck him. Which was when he was broke. He was twenty-four years old. When was he going to settle down, get a job, grow up?

She frowned and headed for her bedroom to change clothes. She prayed he didn't need money this time. He'd promised, after that last business with dog racing, of all things, that he would stop gambling, never ask her for money again. That had been more than a year ago, and so far, he'd kept his word. Maybe all her hard work would pay off and he wouldn't end up just like Daddy after all.

Anna tucked her precious envelope in her purse and placed the purse on her dresser.

What would she do if he was here for money? What would she tell him?

After removing her gray linen skirt and jacket and making sure they hung straight on their hangers, she slipped off her tailored, white cotton blouse, her mind worrying over Ben's arrival. She knew, deep down inside, that he wouldn't have come unless he wanted something from her. And the only thing he ever wanted from her was money. It hurt, but that was Ben.

She slipped on jeans, a cotton shirt, socks and sneakers, then tiptoed past the living room to the kitchen. By the time she had baked a potato in the microwave and tossed herself a salad, she had managed to put her anxiety over Ben from her mind. She would worry about what he wanted when he told her what he wanted.

As soon as she cleaned up the kitchen, she went to the small desk in the corner of the den and filled out the college admission form. Three times during the process, she had to stop and calm herself so her hand wouldn't shake with excitement. She didn't want to take the chance of messing up the form. Not now, when she was finally about to realize her dream.

If her stomach clenched at the thought of the damage Ben could do to her dream, she ignored it. He wasn't in trouble. Not this time. Surely not this time.

Wondering when he'd developed that cute little snore, she left him sleeping on the couch until the next morning. By then she decided he'd slept long enough. She leaned over him and touched his warm, bare shoulder. "You've been sleeping forever. Get up and I'll fix your breakfast."

He shifted and groaned and stretched, one of those quivering, all-over body stretches. Even his bare toes hanging off the end of the couch curled and flexed. With his face still buried in the pillow, he muttered in a deep, gravelly voice, "You're a saint, Mom."

Mom?

Then he rolled over and gave her a slow, lazy grin. Then slowly he opened his eyes.

It was impossible to determine who was more startled, Anna, or the man on her couch. The man she'd never seen before in her life.

With a scream, she jerked away, fell backward over the coffee table, and landed hard on her rear.

The stranger on the couch jumped up and reached across the coffee table toward her. "Are you all right?"

Seeing him lunge toward her, Anna screamed again and shoved against the coffee table with her feet to push herself out of his reach. The sharp edge of the glass top struck him forcefully in the shins, but she was too terrified to appreciate his grunt of pain.

If she tried for the front door she would have to pass right next to him and he'd be able to grab her. If she tried for the back door she'd be trapped in the garage, as the side door stuck and the big door was slow to open.

All of this was assuming her legs would carry her that far in either direction. Since they felt about as substantial as cooked spaghetti, it seemed doubtful.

That left the phone. She had to get to the phone.

"Don't touch me," she warned, her chest heaving, her mind threatening to go blank with fear.

"Okay," he said breathlessly, grabbing his shins as he fell back onto the couch. "Okay. Sorry. I didn't mean to scare you. "Damn," he muttered, rubbing both legs. "That hurt."

She didn't care if she'd broken both his legs. While he was distracted by his pain she pushed herself to her feet and whirled for the wall phone at the end of the kitchen cabinet. She grabbed up the receiver and pressed the nine—

"You don't need to do that," the stranger said in a rush. "My name's Gavin Marshall."

She missed, hit the two, and had to disconnect and start over. Learning his name did nothing to reassure her. Nine—one—

"I'm a friend of your brother's."

By the time his words registered through the static of fear in her head—Ben? The man had something to do with Ben?—it was too late to stop her finger from pressing the one a second time.

She whipped her head around to stare at the stranger who'd invaded her home. He wasn't coming after her as she'd feared. He hadn't even moved from the couch.

With her heart thundering, she stabbed her finger over the switch hook to disconnect the call before the 9-1-1 operator could answer. "How do I know you're Ben's friend?"

The man pulled his wallet from the back pocket of his jeans and tossed it toward her. It landed at her feet. "I guess if he's never mentioned me, I can't prove we're friends, but that should at least prove my identity."

Anna's hands shook as she bent and retrieved the wallet. California driver's license, half a dozen gold and platinum credit cards and some sort of union card all proclaimed him to be who he said he was, Gavin Marshall, of Santa Monica, California.

She compared the driver's license picture to the man across the room. It wasn't fair, she thought, for a man that good-looking to have such a good photo on his license. It looked almost like a studio portrait, the way it showed off those chiseled good looks, his dark, sun-streaked hair, those startlingly blue eyes, a mouth that did funny things to her breathing. He was smiling in the photo. Lord, if he ever smiled at her like that...

What was she thinking? She didn't care what the man's smile looked like. "Where is Ben?"

"I don't know," Marshall said. "But unless he got here before me and has already left, he should be showing up anytime now."

"You mean, you didn't come with him?"

"No."

"No, what?" she snapped, her nerves still frayed despite the lessening of her fear. "No, you didn't mean that, or no, you didn't come with him?"

"No, I didn't come with him."

"Then what are you doing with his motorcycle? What are you doing in my house? How did you get in?"

"Ben gave me his keys."

Anna blinked. "Ben never lets anyone drive that motorcycle. Never."

The man on her couch shrugged. "That's what I thought, too. But he wanted to drive my car, so he gave me his keys. I'm meeting him here to swap back."

"Here? You came all the way from California to swap vehicles with Ben?"

"Yes, ma'am."

Well, if that didn't sound like something Ben would think up—"Hey, buddy, let's meet halfway across the country and trade rides"—nothing did. And as she thought about it, she realized that the name Gavin did ring a bell in the back of her mind. She couldn't remember why, exactly, but it seemed to be something Ben had told her that she, for once, had approved of.

This man must truly be a friend of Ben's. Not one of the creeps he gambled with, but an actual friend.

Relief weakened her knees. Before she could fall to the floor she pulled out a dinette chair and sat. "You scared ten years off my life."

"I'm sorry," he told her. "I didn't mean to fall asleep. When I got in I was hot and tired. I just thought I'd rest for a few minutes..." He leaned over and snagged his T-shirt from atop the duffel bag. When he poked his head through the neck hole he looked around the room and frowned. "Hell, surely I didn't really sleep clear through to Saturday."

"Surely you did," she snapped. Now that her fear was abating—after all, she knew this man, more or less—anger and confusion swamped her. She didn't like being afraid. In fact, she'd never been so terrified in her life as when he'd rolled over and she had realized he wasn't Ben. It made her angry that he had scared her. It made her whopping mad.

The anger was alien to her—Anna didn't normally waste her time or energy on emotions—but it was there and undeniable.

"So when Ben wasn't here," she said hotly, "you just decided to let yourself into my house while no one was home? That's...unconscionable."

At least he had the good grace to look sheepish. "You're right. I shouldn't have done it."

"It was highly presumptuous."

"Yes, ma'am. And rude, and tacky, and unkind to scare you the way I did. I'm sorry. I got in about noon. I was afraid if I hung around on your front porch too long your neighbors might call the police on me."

It was almost the truth, Gavin admitted to himself. As much of the truth as he was willing to give her for the time being.

Damn, he really hadn't meant to scare her half to death. He had to assume her face wasn't always as pale as milk. He'd scared the color clear out of her cheeks. And she was still shaking. Just a little, but enough to see. He didn't much like what her fear said about him. He hadn't come here to terrorize some innocent woman. If she was innocent.

Gavin assumed she was. It would be just like that irresponsible brother of hers to let her take the heat for his shenanigans. In fact, according to what Ben himself had told him more than once, it *was* just like him.

But she wasn't totally blameless. She was the one, Gavin knew, who had taught Ben, through always bailing him out of trouble, that he never had to worry about dealing with the consequences of his own actions. His sister would deal with them for him. According to the stories Ben told—with pride rather than the rueful shame he should have felt—Anna Collins had consistently reinforced Ben's irresponsibility time and time again.

She was Ben's enabler. Like Aunt Marilyn was for Danny. Like the loved one who always covered up and made excuses for the alcoholic, she had only managed to make matters worse.

Scratch innocent. Anna Collins was definitely culpable.

She met his gaze straight-on despite the remnants of fear that darkened those wide gray eyes. She might be at the root of Gavin's current problem, but a man had to admire courage in a woman, especially when she was barely half his size.

"You're right," she told him. "Seeing a man hanging around my front porch all afternoon would probably have sent several of my neighbors to call the police."

"Now it looks like I'll be talking to them anyway."

"My neighbors?"

"The police."

"Why?" She blinked like a baby owl.

"You dialed 9-1-1, didn't you?"

"I hung up before anyone answered."

Gavin shook his head. "It doesn't matter. Once you dial all three numbers, they know who called. They usually send a car anyway just to make sure everything's all right."

Terrific, Anna thought with an inward groan. Just what she needed to make her day complete. The police. Her neighbors were going to love that.

It was barely 9:00 a.m. and she was exhausted. Terror, she assumed, did that to a person. Terror, and anger.

Well, she had time for neither. Regardless of the fact

that Gavin Marshall had scared the wits out of her, he was Ben's friend. She remembered that now. He shouldn't have let himself into her house, but he was here now. The least she could do was show him a little hospitality. Not that she was any good at small talk, but she would give it her best. If, she thought, she could ignore that T-shirt he had pulled on. She remembered enough from Ben's teen years to recognize that the Grateful Dead was the name of a rock group, but while she knew nothing of their music, she found their name distasteful in the extreme.

But since he'd left home six years ago Ben had not brought any of his new friends home. She wanted the chance to know someone he would choose to call friend.

Brushing her hands together as if dusting them off, she rose from the dining table and pushed her chair back in place. "When did Ben say he would be here?"

Gavin pushed himself from the couch and stood, all six foot plus of him. "If he was coming straight here like I thought, he should have been here by Thursday night or Friday morning. Mind if I use your bathroom?"

"Be my guest. It's through that door and to the left." She frowned as she watched his back disappear around the corner into the hall. His wording puzzled her.

"What did you mean," she asked when he came back a few minutes later, "if he came straight here like you thought? I thought you said this was all arranged. Didn't he tell you when to meet him?"

Well, here we go, Gavin thought, rubbing the side of his nose. "Not exactly." He wouldn't lie to her, but she wasn't going to like the truth.

Oh, he did love the way she arched that brow. "Not exactly what?" she asked.

"It wasn't exactly arranged," he admitted.

She folded her arms across her chest. Her eyes narrowed. "I think you'd better explain what's going on, Mr. Marshall. Maybe I was a little hasty in hanging up the phone."

"It's Gavin, and no, you weren't hasty. If I can get my car back from Ben, there won't be any need to involve the police."

"What?" she shrieked. "What are you saying?"

Gavin could have kicked himself. He shouldn't have put it quite that way. But he was damn good and mad at Ben Collins. The kid had gone over the line this time and somebody had to put the fear of God into that young man before he ended up in real trouble. Ben reminded him so much of Danny it was scary. Gavin did not want Ben ending up like Danny. If it took tough measures to prevent it—and it looked like that was exactly what it was going to take—then Gavin would just have to be tough.

"I said I came here to swap vehicles with Ben. That much is true. But the original swap—when he, uh, *borrowed* my car and left me his Harley—was made without my knowledge or consent."

Anna gripped the back of the chair she'd just vacated. Gavin Marshall might have said *borrowed*, but what Anna heard in his voice was something else entirely, something she refused to accept. She forced herself to breathe slowly. "Tell me," she demanded. "Just come out with it and tell me what's going on."

Gavin let out a long breath. "Why don't we sit down?"

"Why don't you just tell me what it is you're trying to avoid telling me?"

Gavin felt as if he were about to go tiptoeing through a minefield, but there was no help for it. He didn't want to chance Ben getting to her with some sob story and her giving her brother the money he needed. This time Ben was going to have to solve his own problems, by damn.

Gavin crossed the room and pulled out a chair at the opposite end of the table from where Anna stood. There he paused and waited.

With a reluctant shrug, she finally pulled out her chair and sat again. "All right, I'm sitting."

Gavin sat and faced her. "First of all, you have to understand that I meant what I said. Ben and I are friends. Good friends."

With a toss of her head, Anna met his gaze squarely. "I assume there's a but."

"Yeah, there's a but. He went too far this time when he took my car."

Anna lowered her gaze to the table rather than look him in the eye any longer. "You've said borrowed, and you've said took."

"He didn't ask, Anna," Gavin said as gently as he could. "He didn't bother asking if he could take my car. He knows I would have said no."

She glanced up at him. "A really good friend, huh? And you wouldn't lend him your car?"

"My '57 Vette?" His voice rose in protest. "Not only no, but hell no. I wouldn't let my own mother drive that car. And Ben knows it."

Anna's stomach tightened. As little as she knew about cars, even she knew that a '57 Corvette was considered a classic. Men, as she understood, were touchy about their toys.

Ben, Ben, what have you done?

The thought made her feel so disloyal that shame washed through her. Ben was just young, just a little irresponsible. He wasn't a bad person. He had a tendency to gamble, but he was more careful these days not to bet money he didn't have. He promised he'd be more careful. He wouldn't do anything really bad. He wouldn't steal a car.

"Ben's not a thief," she said, her voice wavering.

Gavin winced. The look of pain and pleading on her face was almost enough to make a stone weep, and Gavin was no stone. But he couldn't let her get to him. If he softened toward her or Ben on this, it would be Ben who ultimately paid the price.

"He took my keys off my counter when I wasn't looking and left town. He left a message on my voice mail saying he was on his way to get the money he owes me."

Anna's eyes slid closed. Her throat worked up and down on a swallow. "What..." She swallowed again. "What do you want from me? I don't...have much money."

"I wouldn't care if you did. It's your brother I want."

"But you can see he's not here." There was that pain, that pleading again.

"Not yet. But he'll come."

"What makes you say that?"

"Because this is where he always comes when he's in trouble, isn't it?"

Her eyes widened. "How— What makes you say that?"

"Ben. He talks about you to his friends."

The lines of pain on her face deepened, her eyes darkened. "He's not a thief. He's *not.*"

She sounded to Gavin as though she were trying to convince herself rather than him. But he didn't really think Ben Collins was a thief. Ben was younger than any twenty-four-year-old should be. He was irresponsible as hell. And despite having stood on the curb with his mouth hanging open while Ben had taken off in his car, despite Ben still owing him money, Gavin still had trouble believing there was anything malicious or criminal in Ben's makeup.

No, the car was a prank. Ben was good at pranks. Sometimes too good, and this time Gavin was going to teach the little jerk a lesson before he ended up pulling one of his pranks on the wrong person—or borrowing money from the wrong person—and getting himself into more trouble than he could handle.

"A few months ago he borrowed money from me and failed to pay it back at the promised time. Two days ago he stole my car from my driveway and hasn't been seen since. What would you call it?"

The woman stared at him like a rabbit caught in the glare of headlights. "A misunderstanding?"

"Nice try, but no."

"A...a prank?"

Ah, so maybe she did know her brother after all. "A damned expensive prank, wouldn't you say?"

"I wouldn't know. You have his motorcycle. They aren't cheap."

"You should know. I'll bet you paid for most of it. But neither's a '57 Vette."

Slowly her expression changed from pain and fear

to confusion. "How much could a forty-some-year-old car be worth compared to that motorcycle?"

Gavin knew his mouth had fallen open, but for a minute he didn't seem to be able to do anything about it. Then he broke out laughing. "That was a good one," he managed. "For a minute, you really had me going."

Her head tilted to one side as her brow furrowed. "Had you going? I don't understand."

Gavin chuckled and shook his head. "You can't get me twice with the same joke. I'm not that big a sucker."

Her expression changed this time to irritation. "I'm sure I don't have the slightest idea what you're talking about. But since your disagreement is with my brother, and he is obviously not here, I'll thank you to clean up this mess you've made in my living room and vacate my house."

It was Gavin's turn to tilt his head and frown. Mess? He glanced around the living room at the things he'd brought in with him. What mess? He shook his head. "I hate to disappoint you, but I can't leave until Ben shows up."

With her chin jutting out, she rose from the chair and aligned it up against the table where it had been. "There's no reason for you to wait here for him. I'm quite certain they have telephones in Santa Monica."

"So they do. But your little brother knows he's up to his irresponsible little neck in trouble this time, and if there's one thing I know about Ben Collins, it's that when he's in trouble, he runs home to big sister. I'm sorry, Anna, but it looks like you're stuck with me until he gets here."

"You can't mean that!"

"I don't have much choice."

She gaped, her mouth working like a fish out of water. "You can't stay in my house."

"I have to," he told her. "I promise I won't be a bit of trouble. You won't even know I'm around."

Her eyes widened with what could only be horror as she looked at his gear lined up against the wall. "You're not serious. This is a joke. I don't know what kind, but it has to be a joke."

"If it's a joke, I wish somebody would tell me the punch line," he said irritably.

Slowly, with her eyes bulging, she said, one drawn-out word at a time, "Oh...my...word."

"I'm sorry, Anna, but I have to be here when Ben shows up."

"You can't stay here," she said again.

Okay, he thought, grinding his teeth. He'd tried being reasonable, and she wasn't going for it. Not that he could blame her, but he wasn't going to let any of them—her, Ben, nor himself—off easily. It was time to get a little tougher. "Since I outweigh you by at least seventy-five pounds, I don't think there's much you can do about it. I'm not leaving until I know where my car is and until I know that I'm getting it back."

Her spine snapped straight, like the string on a bow that had just fired an arrow. "We'll just see about that." She turned and marched toward the phone again.

"You've already called the police once."

"This time I won't hang up."

A little tougher wasn't getting it, Gavin acknowledged. Anna Collins was not the pushover Ben had led him to believe. He was going to have to bluff, and bluff good. "I haven't filed a stolen car report yet. I don't think you want me to."

She whirled on him. "Am I supposed to just agree to this crazy scheme of yours? For all I know, you're making this whole story up. How do I know you haven't murdered Ben and stolen his motorcycle? How do I know you haven't come here to kill me?"

"I'm likely to if you don't quit calling that bike a motorcycle like it was some ten-horsepower glorified lawn mower. It's a Harley-Davidson, for cryin' out loud. A Harley is not just a motorcycle. I'm not here to murder you, or rape you, or anything else dastardly, and I didn't kill your brother—yet."

Both of her eyebrows climbed upward. "I'm supposed to take the word of a complete stranger who's broken into my house?"

"I didn't break in," he said with disgust. "I have Ben's keys."

Her brows lowered and drew together as she narrowed her eyes. "Yes, you said he left them when he took yours. That sounds very much like a trade to me, rather than grand theft auto."

"It might have been his idea of a trade, but I never agreed to it. He's out joyriding in a very expensive car that doesn't belong to him, and so help me, if he puts so much as a ding in it, I'll wring his neck."

"All this?" she shrieked. "Over an old car?"

"A classic '57 Vette in mint condition is not an *old car.*"

"Have you sought counseling for this unhealthy attachment you have for wheeled vehicles?"

He wasn't going to have any teeth left if he didn't quit grinding them. "Aside from the car itself, there were things in it that I need back."

She planted her hands on her hips.

Nice hips, he thought.

"What kinds of things?" she demanded.

Irritated that he would notice her hips when she was insulting his intelligence, his mental stability and his Vette, he caught himself grinding his teeth again. "The kinds of things that are none of your business."

"I beg to differ. You've accused my brother of a crime, you've barged into my home uninvited—"

"Barging is usually done without an invitation, otherwise it wouldn't be barging, would it? And I've apologized for that a dozen times already."

"You can go stay in a hotel. I'll call you if Ben shows up."

Gavin was shaking his head before she finished. "Anna, I can't do that. If I'm not right here when he shows up, either you'll tell him I'm here and he'll leave, or you'll give him the money to pay me off. I don't want you getting him out of trouble this time. He's past the age when he should be accepting the responsibility for his own actions and not running to you for help all the time."

Anna opened her mouth, then snapped it shut. It was hard to argue with the truth, no matter how much that truth stung.

Outside at the curb, car doors slammed. She glanced out the sheers on the front window and stiffened. *The police.*

What was she going to do? Tell them the truth and risk getting Ben in trouble, or go along with this stranger and pretend nothing was wrong?

Her instinct for survival warned her not to take a chance with her own safety. For all she knew, Gavin Marshall could be a serial killer on a cross-country spree.

But another instinct even stronger, the instinct to

protect her brother, rose up in her, along with a voice in the back of her head. Both told her that Gavin Marshall was telling the truth, and that he would not harm her.

The man looked determined enough, big enough to do anything. Dare she trust that voice in her head?

Yet there was that faint memory of Ben telling her what a good influence his friend Gavin was, how much he looked up to the man, how much the man was helping him get his act together.

That didn't sound like a man who'd come here to harm her. Did it?

Before she could decide, two police officers stepped onto her front porch and rang her doorbell.

Chapter Two

As the sound of the doorbell faded, Gavin leveled a look at her. "Don't leave me without a choice, Anna. I don't want to turn him in, but I'm not going to let you get me arrested, either."

When Anna merely stood there staring at him, trying to decide what to do, he stepped past her and opened the door. With a rueful smile, he pushed open the storm door. "I told her she hung up too late, that you'd come anyway."

"Is there a problem?" one officer asked.

Anna stepped up beside Gavin.

"Ms. Collins."

"Officer Wilkins."

"Oh, ho," Gavin laughed. "I didn't realize you were on a last-name basis with the local police."

Anna spared him a glare.

"And you are?" Officer Wilkins asked.

Gavin stuck out his hand. "Gavin Marshall. I have to take the blame for Anna dialing 9-1-1."

"How's that?"

Gavin's grin was so sheepish, Anna ground her teeth. "Her brother and I traded vehicles and I'm meeting him here to trade back. Since I have Ben's keys, I let myself in while she was out. When she walked in, she thought I was a burglar. She'd already dialed 9-1-1 before I could explain."

The policeman pursed his lips and raised an eyebrow at Anna. "Is that so?"

Anna had to hand it to Gavin. He had told the literal truth. And he'd given the police his name. That had to mean he had no plans to harm her, for if anything happened to her they'd know who to look for.

Of course, by then she'd be dead or raped or mangled or whatever, but they would know who to look for.

Don't be a ninny. The man's had plenty of time to do you harm if he'd wanted to. He's been here all night and you slept like a baby. If he was here to hurt you, he could have killed you in your sleep.

A comforting thought, being killed in her sleep. Still, he had certainly had the opportunity. Instead he'd chosen to sleep. It wasn't her he was after, it was Ben.

She gave Officer Wilkins a hesitant nod. "I wasn't expecting him. I'm sorry you had to come over here for nothing."

Officer Wilkins visibly relaxed. "No problem. We just wanted to make sure everything was all right. How is your brother doing these days? Is he staying out of trouble?"

Anna fought to keep from bristling. Just because the neighbors had called the police on Ben a time or two,

Wilkins didn't have to make it sound as though her brother were constantly in trouble. And Gavin didn't have to wear such an irritatingly blank look on his face, as if he were trying to keep from gloating. "Ben's fine," she said tersely.

As the officers turned to go, Wilkins paused and looked back at Anna's unwanted houseguest. "You're riding his Harley?"

"It's in the garage."

"For the sake of your traffic record, I hope you don't tear up the streets with it the way young Collins does when he hits town. There's not a cop around who doesn't know that bike."

"I'll keep that in mind, Officer."

"You do that."

When the officers reached their car, Anna closed the front door.

Gavin touched her arm. "Thank you."

Anna scowled and shook off his touch. "For what, being a wuss?"

He laughed. "You're no wuss, Anna Collins, and I've got the bruises on my shins to prove it."

"If you expect me to apologize for that, do me a favor and hold your breath while you wait."

He laughed again. "I don't expect an apology. In your place I would have done the same thing. Why don't you let me make it up to you by taking you out to breakfast?"

Anna had been about to walk away, but she paused. She had always been taught that everyone had a price. It was to her shame that hers was a free meal cooked by someone else. She had learned that back in the days after her parents' deaths, when she had worked two, sometimes three jobs to keep the wolves away from the door. A free meal back then had been a godsend. Sometimes it meant the difference between eating, or going hungry.

Twelve years later she was still counting her pennies, but she could afford to feed herself. Still, the thought of a free meal out was a temptation she was loathe to refuse.

"Aha," Gavin said. "I think I just found the key to your heart."

"You should be so lucky."

Not me, Gavin thought. Some other man would surely win the heart of Anna Collins someday, but it wouldn't be Gavin Marshall.

Not that there was anything wrong with her.

Well, not much, anyway, except that she was her brother's enabler. That aside, she was smart, courageous, stubborn. Yeah, he even liked that stubbornness. And she damn sure wasn't hard on the eyes, either. She stood about five-four, maybe a hundred and twenty pounds. Maybe less. Her hair was the color of raw honey. It just teased the line of her jaw and framed her oval face perfectly, highlighting a pair of gray eyes wide enough for a man to drown in and be glad when he went down for the third time.

Yeah, some man was going to be damn lucky when he found the key to her heart.

Gavin, on the other hand, was not looking for that kind of luck. He liked his life just the way it was, liked being able to come and go as he pleased without worrying about what anyone else might think or need. Footloose and freewheeling, that was him. He liked his women like he liked his vacations—exciting, adventurous and temporary.

Anna Collins was not the temporary type. She had

home and hearth, commitment and permanence written all over her.

No, sir, not for him. He didn't want the key to her heart.

"Okay," he said with a grin. "Maybe a breakfast out is the key to your forgiveness for my barging in on you. I'll even let you wear the helmet."

Her eyes widened. "And why," she said slowly, "would I need a helmet in my own car?"

"Uh-uh. I said I was taking you. That means the Harley."

For Anna, it was no contest. A free meal was not worth it. "I'll cook."

"What's this? I thought you wanted to go out."

She turned away and headed for the kitchen. "Not if it means riding that growling beast."

"You don't like riding the Harley?" he said, astounded.

Anna bristled. "I hate to disappoint you, but I also don't like baseball or hot dogs. To my credit, I do love apple pie, and I fly the American flag on all the appropriate holidays. How does bacon and eggs sound?"

Anna carefully added another strip of bacon to the skillet. It occurred to her, as she called herself every kind of fool for cooking breakfast for a man she didn't want in her house, that she was no longer afraid of Gavin Marshall. He'd had ample opportunity to harm her, rob her, or anything else he might have wanted to do.

Instead he'd done nothing but talk to her. He'd even gone to the door and let the police see him. He'd given them his name.

Okay, so maybe he wasn't here to murder her. She

still didn't want him in her house. She didn't want him lying in wait to catch Ben unawares. Although if Gavin was telling the truth, it was nothing more than Ben deserved.

Ben, what am I supposed to do with this man?

The only thing she knew to do was to try to get him to leave before Ben came. Then she could talk to Ben and find out just what the devil he thought he was doing.

She added the final slice of bacon to the skillet, then reached for the bread box. They would have toast.

Yes, she wanted Gavin Marshall out of her house.

After preparing the bread for the toaster oven, she cracked four—better make that six—eggs into a bowl and added grated cheddar. The thought of having slept the entire night while a strange man sprawled on her couch unnerved her.

A few minutes later she set everything on the table. Still trying to figure out a way to convince Gavin to leave, she sat and started filling her plate.

She needn't have worried about not calling him to the table. He joined her immediately and took his seat. "Damn, this looks great. Like something my mother would fix me."

"And do you have a mother, Mr. Marshall?"

"I have a jewel of a mother. And my name is Gavin."

"I wonder what your mother would say if she knew you'd forced your way into a woman's home and refused to leave, Mr. Marshall."

"I'm sure she'd have a nice, long lecture for me. Got any salt, sugar?"

"My name," she said tightly, "is Anna Collins. You may call me Ms. Collins. The salt is in the cabinet to the right of the stove, Mr. Marshall. What's her phone number?''

He rose and went into the kitchen. Anna refused to watch him. She heard the cabinet door open and close. Then the refrigerator.

Make yourself at home, she thought, jamming a forkful of scrambled eggs into her mouth.

''Whose phone number?'' He returned to the table with the salt and pepper shakers and a jar of her homemade strawberry preserves. ''Mom's?''

''Unless, of course, they don't let her receive calls.''

In the process of ladling strawberry preserves onto a piece of toast, he looked up and frowned. ''What's that supposed to mean, 'they don't let her receive calls'?''

Anna gave him a mock smile. ''From what little I know of you, I can only assume that the poor woman who raised you is either in a mental institution, or in prison.''

The man chuckled. ''You're mean, Anna Collins. I like that. But I have to disappoint you. Mom's more normal than any person I know.''

''But you're not going to give me her phone number.''

But he did give her the phone number. Or *a* phone number, she thought. As fast as he rattled it off, and noting no doubt that she had nothing with which to write it down, he probably assumed the number would do her no good. But numbers were Anna's thing. They imprinted themselves onto her brain like newsprint on Silly Putty. She remembered the license number of the old car her parents had driven, the phone number at their house in Lawton before they'd moved to the Oklahoma City area right after Ben was born, and the number of her father's safe-deposit box she'd found after her parents' death. The empty safe-deposit box. She figured she could manage to remember a phone number long enough to stand up and dial the phone.

When she finished eating a few silent moments later, she carried her dishes to the sink, rinsed them and put them in the dishwasher. Then she reached for the phone and punched in the number he'd given her.

"Change your mind about the police?"

Listening to the phone ring at the other end of the line, Anna bit back a smile at the look of apprehension on Gavin Marshall's face.

"Hello?" said a woman on the other end of the line.

Anna gripped the receiver in her suddenly damp palm. "I'm calling for Mrs. Marshall."

Gavin paused with his spoon halfway to his mouth, his eyes wide with surprise.

"You've found me," came the pleasant voice on the other end of the phone.

"Mrs. Marshall, my name is Anna Collins. There's a man in my house who says he's your son."

"Uh-oh." Mrs. Marshall chuckled. "Why do I get the impression that you're not calling to thank me for that?"

Anna couldn't help but smile. "I'm merely trying to ascertain that he is who he says he is."

On the other end of the line, Mrs. Marshall gave a good-natured groan. "It must be Gavin. John and Michael, bless their hearts, have never caused me a moment's concern. What's he done this time?"

"Nothing serious." Oddly, Anna felt compelled to reassure the woman. "Would you mind describing him?"

"Describing him? You mean you don't know—

Never mind. Let's see. He's six feet tall, dark brown hair, although if he's been swimming lately it's probably streaked. Big blue eyes that'll melt your heart. Unless, of course, he's excited or angry. Then they get all wild-looking and make you think he's depraved,'' she added with a laugh.

Involuntarily, Anna looked up from winding the phone cord around her finger and ran smack into those big blue eyes. They most assuredly did not melt her heart. How ridiculous. If her heart was pounding, it was because a stranger had barged into her home. The slight shiver that raced down her backbone was, if not quite fear, then trepidation. Certainly not because of a pair of big blue eyes.

As for depraved…yes. That, she could see.

''And a smile that'll take your breath away.'' A mother's love came through clearly across the line.

Anna's gaze, without her permission, dropped to his mouth. His smiling mouth. Her breath hitched in her chest. *Trepidation.* Only that.

''Does that sound like him?''

Anna jerked her gaze from him and turned toward the wall where the phone was mounted. ''Uh, more or less. Thank you. I hope I haven't disturbed you.''

''Of course you haven't, dear. Gavin is all right, isn't he?''

''Yes. Yes, he's fine.'' It only then dawned on Anna that she might have alarmed the poor woman. ''Would you like to speak with him?''

''Very much. But wait. Did you say your name was Anna Collins?''

''Yes, ma'am.''

''From…oh, where did he say…Oklahoma, that's it. Are you by any chance from Oklahoma?''

"As a matter of fact, I am, but how—"

"You must be Ben's sister," the woman exclaimed with delight. "This is a pleasant surprise indeed."

Anna's heart fluttered. "You know Ben?"

"Oh, my, yes. Let's see…he came up here once a few months ago with Gavin. Yes, I remember now, that was the second time we met him. The first time was last summer when we went to visit Gavin for a week. Ben was so nice and polite."

"I'm relieved to hear it."

Mrs. Marshall chuckled. "And I'm relieved to hear that Gavin finally decided to pay you a visit. I've heard him say several times that he wanted to meet Ben's sister."

"Is that so?"

"Yes, it is. And I want to thank you for calling me. I'm glad to know where he is. He doesn't call often enough to suit me."

"I'm sure he doesn't. Hold on just a minute and I'll put him on." Anna held the phone out to Gavin.

Whatever doubts Anna might have still harbored that Gavin was a good friend of Ben's had just been dispelled by Mrs. Marshall.

"Hey, Mom, how ya doin'? …No, no, it's nothing like that. I came looking for Ben and just sort of took her by surprise, that's all. How's Dad? …Hey, all right! Way to go, Dad. You tell him I said so. And tell Uncle Mick he owes me twenty bucks… Of course I did."

It occurred to Anna as she listened to Gavin talk with his mother that she was being rude to eavesdrop so blatantly. Not that he wasn't being rude to invade her home, friend of Ben's or not, but Gavin's rudeness did not excuse hers. While he finished his conversation, she started cleaning the kitchen.

What a strange man, she thought. He sounded so ordinary when talking to his mother. Just like a regular person, with a mother and father and uncle. Not like an intruder. Not like a man who forced his presence on a woman, right in her own home.

Maybe he was more like Ben than he wanted to admit. Hadn't she just heard him say that he'd won money from his own uncle?

"How about that," he said when he hung up the phone. "Dad finally beat Uncle Mick at golf."

"And you gambled on it, I gather."

"Damn right I did. Uncle Mick's been beating Dad for years. He bragged that even if Dad took lessons from a pro, he'd still beat him. So Dad went out and took lessons and I told Uncle Mick to put his money where his mouth was."

He said it all with such good humor that Anna knew she'd been right. He was a great deal like Ben. Anyone who could laugh about gambling... At least Ben hadn't laughed about it. Not in front of her, anyway. Not like Daddy use to.

Now she had to add swearing to Gavin Marshall's list of shortcomings. Intruder, gambler, curser, slob— her living room was still strewn with his belongings.

"What does that look mean?" he asked.

Anna took her rubber gloves from beneath the sink and started putting them on. "What look?"

"That pursed-lip look you're wearing. Reminds me of my third grade teacher when she caught me chewing gum in class."

Anna refused to dignify such a comment by answering. She also refused, in a moment of decision, to let this man disrupt her life. Perhaps she couldn't physically force him to leave her house, but if she ignored him, maybe he would get bored and leave on his own.

She did her best. Saturday was housecleaning and laundry day. She tackled her chores and completely ignored Gavin Marshall.

Well, as completely as she could. She found it impossible to totally ignore a stranger in her living room.

While she was scrubbing the bathtub, she heard the television come on. When she carried the bathroom cleaning supplies back to the kitchen—just why *did* she keep them beneath the kitchen sink instead of in the bathroom, which was the only place they were used?— she noticed he'd tuned in a baseball game.

It figured. Nothing educational or uplifting for him. He probably read comic books. If he read anything at all.

Shortly after one, she was on her second load of laundry and had done everything but run the vacuum. She took a break for lunch and made herself a tuna sandwich.

Within thirty seconds of taking the lid off the plastic bowl that held her tuna, egg and mayonnaise mixture, Gavin appeared at her elbow and sniffed.

He must have the nose of a bloodhound, she thought with disgust.

"Got enough of that for two?"

"Sorry." Of course, she had plenty, but she deliberately spread the layer of tuna twice as thick as usual and used it all up on her single sandwich while he watched with a pitiful, hangdog expression. "I only keep enough food in the house for one."

He shrugged and smiled. "Makes sense to me, since there's only one of you. I'll just run out and grab something."

"I thought you said you couldn't leave, in case Ben came while you were gone?"

He snapped his fingers. "You're right. Thanks for reminding me."

Anna wanted to kick herself. How stupid could she be, for heaven's sake?

"I'll tell you what," he said. "I'll give you a breather from my presence while I go get something to eat, if you'll make me a promise."

He was going to leave? He was really going to leave, if even for only a few minutes? "What promise is that?"

"You have to promise that if Ben comes while I'm gone, you give me thirty minutes to get back before you tell him I'm in town."

"Sure. Why not?"

"Look at you," he said with disgust. "Don't ever play poker, Anna. Everything you're thinking shows in your eyes."

Anna tossed her head and looked away, hating the fire that stung her cheeks. "I don't know what you're talking about."

"I'm talking about you agreeing to give me thirty minutes when you have no intention of actually doing it. Anna, I'm not the only one Ben owes money to."

Anna quailed. *Ben, what have you done?*

"Look. I'm gonna carry my things in and put them in Ben's closet, so if he comes in while I'm gone he won't see them right off."

Anna watched him do as he said, all the while wondering what she would do if Ben did come while Gavin was gone. Not telling him Gavin was here would be the same as lying. She would be springing a trap on her own brother.

Gavin came, keys in hand, and stood in front of her. "Thirty minutes, Anna, that's all I'm asking. Just thirty minutes."

"I'll...I'll try. That's the best I can offer you. But if he asks me right-out, I won't lie to him."

Gavin nodded once. "Fair enough. You want me to bring you back something?"

"No." She shook her head. "Thank you."

When he left, Anna made sure to lock the door behind him. Then, because she hoped Ben's key ring didn't contain keys to all her locks, she locked all the doors including the big garage door, and their dead bolts, except for the garage door to the kitchen, which didn't have one. She even locked the front storm door and hooked the security chain on the front door. It was worth a try, although she didn't hold out much hope that it would keep Gavin Marshall out.

What she would say to Ben if he came, she still didn't know.

She didn't have to worry about it. Twenty-five minutes later Gavin was back. Locking all the doors did not keep him out. He opened the garage door and parked Ben's motorcycle there, then jiggled the doorknob to the kitchen. A moment later she heard a key slide into the lock, and in he came.

"Nice try," he said. "Don't look so disappointed. I told you I had Ben's keys."

With nothing to say to him, Anna turned on her heel and went to her room, where she closed the door.

There was no lock on her bedroom door. That had never troubled her before. Now it did. Not that she thought Gavin would come into her room, but if she couldn't get him out of her house, she wanted to be able to lock him out of her room.

* * *

Gavin felt like a Class-A jerk. Obviously he hadn't thought this harebrained scheme through very well, nor had he considered the ramifications. It had never been his intent to scare Ben's sister. He wouldn't mind scaring a little sense into Ben, but Anna...

On the other hand, the way Gavin heard it, it was Anna, by always bailing Ben out of trouble, who had taught her brother that he didn't need to bother with taking responsibility for his own actions. Anna took that responsibility for him. If she'd practiced a little tough love and left Ben to extract himself from a mess or two, maybe the kid would have learned by now that life was a little bit more than one big party thrown for his enjoyment.

"Listen to me," Gavin muttered to himself as he flopped onto Anna's couch. Was he any better? In certain circles, Gavin himself was known as quite the partier. But he'd grown up. He'd learned the hard way, watching his cousin barrel down the road to ruin. Gavin would like to spare Ben a possible painful lesson if he could.

But for now he'd better be finding a way to make peace with Anna Lee Collins and convince her that he meant only good for Ben in the long run.

With her arms wrapped around her waist, Anna paced beside her bed, wondering what to do about Gavin Marshall, about Ben.

She couldn't do anything about Gavin's car, but maybe if she offered to pay him the money Ben owed him...

A deep, wrenching pain tore through her at the

thought of giving up her dream of college to get Ben out of trouble—again.

"Ben, why? Why do you do things like this?" *Why do I keep paying for your mistakes?*

She paused at the foot of her bed and waited for the pain to ease. Prayed for a numbness to settle over her so she wouldn't think about college or Ben or the stranger in her living room.

What was she supposed to do now that she had finished her chores? She heard the television through the wall. Was she supposed to spend the rest of the day watching baseball with a stranger?

Groceries. How could she have forgotten?

Gavin Marshall, that's how.

Never mind Gavin Marshall. Saturday wasn't only for cleaning and laundry, it was also grocery day.

With something definite to do, Anna felt better. She squared her shoulders and turned toward her closet. She couldn't go to the store dressed in her housecleaning clothes.

When she left her room fifteen minutes later her hair was neatly combed and she'd donned a pale blue cotton pantsuit, clean tennis shoes and white socks. Her purse hung from the crook in her arm—she'd double-checked to make sure she had her checkbook—and her keys were in her hand.

She came up short at the sight of her intruder sitting on her couch with his elbows braced on spread knees. For a few blessed moments as she had changed clothes she'd forgotten his presence.

He looked up at her and smiled. "Going somewhere?" He glanced down at the keys in her hand, then back up at her face. "Don't leave on my account."

Anna's mouth tightened of its own accord. "If you must know, I'm going grocery shopping."

"Good. I'll go with you."

"No, thank you. But there is something you can do for me."

"Name it."

She smiled. "Be gone when I get back."

"Ah, come on." He rose and propped his hands at his waist. "You know I can't do that."

"Won't, you mean."

"All right, won't. Look, Anna, why don't we call a truce here? I don't want anything from you. I don't mean you any harm at all. If my mother wasn't enough to convince you I'm really a nice guy, I'll give you a list of references as long as your arm. All I want is to be here when Ben shows up."

Anna stared at him a long moment. "What if," she said slowly, "I promise to call you as soon as Ben gets here?"

He was shaking his head before she'd finished. "No dice, darlin'."

"Don't call me that."

"Okay. Ms. Collins. But you know as well as I do that your brother will come breezing in here with some cock-and-bull story to make you feel sorry for him, and the next thing you know you'll be offering to pay off his debt for him."

Anna did her best to stifle a shudder. "And if I did offer?"

"No way, lady. You're not the one who owes me money. I don't want you paying me. I don't want you loaning Ben the money to pay me. That little weasel got himself into this mess without your help. It's past time he grew up, don't you think?"

"I will not discuss my brother's character—"

"Or lack of it."

"—With you. I certainly have no objection to Ben handling his own problems. But I do have an objection to your being in my house. You've no right to be here."

"That's true. I don't. And I'll apologize again for barging in on you, as well as for any inconvenience my presence might cause. But I'm not leaving. Somebody's got to teach that brother of yours a lesson before he lands himself in big-time trouble. It's pretty obvious that someone's not going to be you, or you'd have done it long before now and we wouldn't be having this conversation."

Anna reared back. "You're blaming me for your presence in my home?"

Gavin steeled himself. He had to be tough, mean even. He had to make her believe. "Maybe. I guess I'm suggesting that if you had stopped bailing him out of trouble years ago, he might have learned to stand on his own two feet by now."

Heat flushed across Anna's face. Oh! The man made her so *angry*. Anna wasn't used to anger.

Especially self-directed, said a little voice in the back of her mind. The little voice that told her there was much more truth in Gavin Marshall's last comment than she cared to hear.

"I believe," she told him, "this conversation has come to an end. Don't be here when I get back." She marched past him toward the kitchen, then remembered her car wasn't in its usual spot in the garage. Flushing with renewed, alien anger, she spun on her heel and stomped out the front door.

Gavin bit the inside of his jaw and watched her

blush. All right, if he couldn't talk sense into her, he'd have to try getting past her guard some other way. Remembering the lack of anything much to eat in her kitchen, he decided on his next step.

When Anna backed out of her driveway and pulled up at the corner stop sign two houses away, a black Harley rumbled up behind her with its distinctive, deep-throated growl.

Anna's heart gave a little leap. It was him! Was he really leaving? Weakness flooded her. It was relief. Surely it was relief.

But some tiny little part of her brain whispered, *Disappointment.*

That was ridiculous. She couldn't possibly be disappointed because the stranger in her house was leaving, just the way she told him to.

So what if finding a stranger on her couch was the most excitement she'd ever known? It wasn't exciting, it was terrifying. So maybe he was a handsome man with a pleasing smile and attractive eyes. Danger radiated from Gavin Marshall in waves. Her body picked up the signals and shortened her breath, made her heart pound, weakened her knees.

Danger.

And now he was leaving. Her world would tilt back to its normal angle and life would get back to its usual sameness.

Dullness, you mean.

Anna pushed the thought away.

Admit it. Finding a good-looking stranger on your couch is the most excitement you've ever had.

She pushed that thought away, too. She couldn't

deny the truth of it, but it didn't matter. It was best that he left. Best for Ben, best for her.

Traffic cleared on the cross street. With a final farewell glance in her rearview mirror, Anna pulled away from the stop sign and took her usual route down Northwest Sixty-third to the grocery store.

Chapter Three

A glance in her rearview mirror a moment later had Anna sucking in her breath.

Gavin Marshall was still behind her.

There was something mysterious about the way those mirrored sunglasses hid his eyes from view. Something wild about him, about the way he gripped the handlebars or whatever they were called, the way he straddled the motorcycle, pulling those worn jeans tight over his thighs, the way the wind whipped his hair back from his face.

The latter image burned into her mind when she pulled her gaze from the mirror and once again watched where she was going. It occurred to her that he'd left Ben's helmet behind. Then it occurred to her that he surely hadn't had time to pack all his belongings before he'd left the house.

There was a conclusion she should draw, she knew,

but as it wasn't the one she wanted, she denied what she knew to be true and hoped for the best as she turned in at the parking lot of the grocery store.

He turned in right behind her.

Finally her brain admitted the truth. Gavin Marshall, the man who had invaded her home, the man who wanted to get his hands on her brother, was not leaving town. He was following her. It was enough to make her want to swear.

With her hands clenched tightly around the steering wheel, she pulled into a parking space. By the time she got out of the car and locked it, he was standing at the door to the store, waiting for her. She took one step toward the store and a hot gust of wind slapped her from behind and stood her hair straight up on end.

Mortified, Anna reached to smooth it down. A moment later she scolded herself. She wasn't one to worry about a little thing like windblown hair. Why should she care what she looked like to this man?

She didn't. And that was that.

Shoulders squared, purse hanging from the crook of her arm, she marched straight up to him. "Why have you followed me?" she demanded.

He placed a hand on his chest and gave her a mock look of innocence. "You don't think I expect you to buy my groceries for me, do you? What kind of man do you take me for? No." He held up a hand and grinned. "Never mind. Don't answer that. I'm sure I wouldn't like your answer."

Anna blinked. "If you think buying my groceries is going to—"

"I didn't say I was buying your groceries. I came to buy my own."

"Why do you need groceries if you expect Ben to show up any minute?"

"Because if he doesn't show up by suppertime, I'll get hungry?"

She pursed her lips.

"Okay, how's this? I'm buying Ben's groceries, and until he shows up I'm helping myself." He stepped aside, bent slightly at the waist, and extended an arm toward the automatic door. "After you, ma'am."

In her job as a bookkeeper, and at home living alone, Anna didn't have much call to get angry. She wasn't used to feeling the sting of it rise from inside. Yet how many times this day had she felt like kicking something? Or, more accurately, *someone?*

She clamped her teeth over the petty words that wanted to spew from her lips and entered the store. She would simply ignore him. She couldn't think of anything else to do.

But the man named Gavin Marshall proved impossible to ignore. When she got a shopping cart and started toward the household goods aisle, saving, as she always did, the dairy and produce aisles for last because it took her a half hour to get warm after traversing those cold sections, Gavin Marshall got his own shopping cart and followed her.

She breathed a sigh of relief when he stopped at the book and magazine racks. Quickly she turned her cart down the detergent aisle and hefted a large bottle into her cart, then moved on. She was in the Sundries aisle, looking at razors, when he strolled by and stopped at the selection of men's shaving creams.

Anna would have ignored him. She meant to. But she couldn't help but stare at the lone item in his shopping cart. As far as she knew, she'd never met a grown man who read comic books.

"If you're nice," he said as he plucked a can of shaving cream off the shelf and used it to point at the comic book, "I'll let you read it after me."

Anna turned abruptly away and grabbed the first package of razors she reached, then pushed her cart down the aisle.

On Cereals, she bought Shredded Wheat. He bought Froot Loops and Frosted Flakes.

On Canned Goods, she bought tomato paste. He bought chili and peaches.

She skipped Soft Drinks, but when next she saw him he'd added three liters of Coke to his basket.

Apparently he knew her brother's tastes quite well.

When he reached for a six-pack of Coors on a large end display, she cleared her throat loudly. "Ben doesn't drink in my house."

"These," he said with a smug smile, "are for me."

"You," she answered with a smile even more smug, "don't drink in my house, either."

He frowned. "I don't?"

She frowned more fiercely. "You don't."

With the expression of a young boy bidding a final farewell to his best friend, Gavin put the six-pack back.

On the Bakery aisle, she bought whole-wheat bread and plain bagels. He bought white bread and a large package of cinnamon rolls.

She bypassed the frozen food section. He loaded up with frozen dinners, Häagen-Dazs ice cream and fish sticks.

At the Meat counter she picked out boneless, skinned chicken breasts, a lean chuck roast and three pounds of extra-lean ground beef she would have to separate into one-pound packages when she got home.

Gavin passed her and stopped at the lunch meat case, where he selected bologna and hot dogs, then turned back toward her. "I don't suppose you have any mustard— Never mind. I'll get some."

She made it to the Dairy case and bought four cartons of fat-free yogurt in various flavors, a half-gallon of skimmed milk, "heart-smart" margarine and a pint of low-fat cottage cheese. She didn't see Gavin again until the checkout stands, where he stood in line behind a woman with two small children and enough food in her cart to prepare for a lengthy siege. He'd added two dozen eggs, a pound of bacon and three bags of chocolate chip cookies to his cart.

Anna ignored him and pushed her cart in behind a woman buying a potted plant and a package of ground beef, thinking, rather smugly, she admitted, that she would be checked out and on her way home before he ever got his cart emptied onto the conveyor belt.

Things didn't happen quite that way. Upon close inspection the philodendron the woman ahead of her had chosen sported a healthy population of aphids. It just wouldn't do. Rather than give up her place in line to go pick out a new plant, the customer insisted that the clerk send someone to select a replacement for her. Her hip ached and she didn't want to walk back to the plant display area again.

A sack boy chose a new plant, same type, same size. But the foil paper around the pot was the wrong color.

Anna took long, deep breaths as the drama played out slowly in front of her and the margarine in her basket approached room temperature. At the next register, the woman with the two children paid her total and led the way out the door while a sack girl followed with a cart filled with the woman's bagged purchases.

Gavin loaded his items onto the conveyor belt, and the checker whipped them past the scanner faster than a springtime tornado. By the time he sauntered out the door with the loose-hipped gait of an Old West gunslinger, the woman in front of Anna finally wrote her check.

It occurred to Anna, as her groceries were being checked and bagged, to wonder how Gavin was going to get his groceries home on the motorcycle.

When she left the store a few minutes later, followed by the sacker pushing her cart of purchases, she had her answer. Gavin Marshall wasn't going to get his groceries home on the motorcycle. Grinning, he stood next to her car and waited for her, obviously expecting her to haul them home for him.

"I knew you wouldn't mind," he told her.

Anna had the strident urge to grab his plastic bags and fling their contents across the parking lot.

The urge unsettled her. She was not a violent person. She'd never been prone to anger before meeting this man. With controlled effort, she slipped her key into the lock on her trunk and turned it. Standing aside while her bags were moved from the shopping cart into her trunk, she said not a word when Gavin loaded his bags in beside hers. She very much feared that if she opened her mouth, something totally unladylike would escape.

Anna thanked the sacker, then slipped into her car and drove home.

Gavin followed close behind her. He was really starting to like this woman. It probably wasn't very nice of him to enjoy getting a rise out of her, but there it was. She was fun to rile.

As long, he thought, as it wasn't over anything serious, such as her feelings of safety. As long as he wasn't causing her genuine distress. That, he didn't want.

No, he only wanted two things from Anna Collins. He wanted her to stop bailing Ben out of trouble, and he wanted her to not be angry with Gavin for forcing his company on her the way he was doing.

Yeah, well, pal, you go ahead and want in one hand...

When Anna pulled into her driveway and started to get out to open the garage door, Gavin blocked her car door with the Harley.

"I'll get the door," he called over the throaty rumble of the motorcycle's engine and the louder clatter of her car.

Well, Anna thought, at least he was making himself useful.

When he raised the garage door, she pulled her car in, killed the engine and got out.

"If you park in the middle like that, I can't get the Harley in."

Anna raised an eyebrow at him. "And your point is..."

"Of course, it's not my bike, so if it gets stolen out of your driveway, it's no skin off my nose. I guess it's insured. Although if anyone is paying insurance premiums on it, it would have to be you, so you'd know that better than I would."

With a slow, deep breath for patience, Anna climbed back into the car, backed it out, and pulled in again, this time leaving room for the motorcycle on her passenger side. While Gavin pulled in, she unlocked her trunk and reached for her bags.

"I'll get those."

Well. Useful indeed. When Ben was home, he certainly never offered to carry in the groceries.

She pulled two bags from the trunk herself and carried them into the kitchen. Turning from the counter to go back for more, she nearly ran into Gavin. He had carried in the rest of her bags, and all of his, at once.

"You really ought to get an automatic garage door opener." He set the bags on the counter and untangled his hands from the plastic handles.

"I'm perfectly capable of opening my own garage door."

He started emptying the contents of the bags onto the counter. "Of course you are. But wouldn't it be easier if you didn't have to?"

"Easier? Is that what you look for, the easy way?"

"You sure are prickly."

"What's that supposed to mean?"

"It means you'd rather do things the hard way than admit somebody else had a good idea."

"I don't know why you would say something like that. You know nothing about me."

"I know you'd rather get out in the rain and lift that heavy door yourself than admit how convenient a garage door opener would be."

"In case you failed to notice, it's not raining."

"Prickly, and stubborn."

Anna placed her milk, margarine, cottage cheese and yogurt in the refrigerator. "What do you do for a living, Mr. Marshall, that makes you think money should be wasted on luxuries like garage door openers?"

"Luxuries?" he protested. "An automatic garage

door opener stopped being a luxury back in the seventies. If you don't care about the convenience, how about the safety aspect? You won't throw your back out, and some mugger can't grab you from behind while you're out opening the door.''

Anna took her time carefully placing the chicken and roast in the freezer, setting the three-pound package of ground beef in the sink for dividing and rewrapping. It was either place all items with care, or risk giving in to the urge to throw them. A mugger, indeed. Did he get a commission on automatic garage door openers or something?

''You know what they call people like you who refuse to take precautions?''

''No, but I'm sure you're going to tell me.''

''Victims.''

Anna slammed the freezer door closed and whirled to face him. ''I'm nobody's victim, Mr. Marshall.''

''Don't kid yourself. You're your own brother's favorite victim.''

''How dare you say such a thing!''

''You do know you're the reason he never worries about getting himself into trouble, don't you? He knows you'll always bail him out. Is that why you don't have something as basic as a garage door opener? You spend all your money bailing Ben out of trouble?''

''If—and right now that's a very big if—I'm not going to call the police again and have you forcibly removed from my home, you're going to have to keep your opinions about my relationship with my brother to yourself.''

''Look. I like Ben. He's basically a good kid. All I'm saying is that he's never learned to take responsibility for his own actions, because he knows you'll take the responsibility for him.''

It was hard to argue against the truth, and Anna resented Gavin all the more for speaking it so plainly. She *did* take the responsibility for Ben's actions on herself. She *did* keep bailing him out of trouble. She couldn't help it. Ben was all she had left, her only family.

''Whatever is between Ben and me is none of your business.''

''When he starts pulling his little stunts on me, I make it my business.''

This wasn't going to work, Anna realized. Gavin was obviously not going to leave on his own—he'd just bought enough groceries for a week.

Ben, Ben, when are you going to grow up and stop getting us into these messes?

No answer came, and she felt disloyal for asking the question. For too many years it had been her and Ben against the world. Or the world against her and Ben. She could not stop protecting her brother merely because she knew she should, or because Gavin Marshall told her to.

Resigned to the inevitable, she took a slow, deep breath and faced the man in her kitchen. ''How much money does Ben owe you?''

Gavin's eyes narrowed as he studied her. ''Oh, no, you don't. You're not going to get him off the hook by paying me yourself. This is exactly what I came here to prevent.''

''How much?''

''Nothin' doin', doll. I won't take your money. It's not your debt, it's Ben's. Make him own up to it, Anna. Make him pay it himself.''

"How much, Gavin?"

"How the hell's he ever going to learn that his actions have consequences that he has to face on his own if you keep bailing him out?"

"How much?"

"Forty-five thousand dollars."

Ann grabbed for the counter to keep from falling down.

Chapter Four

"Forty-fi—"

"More like forty-six," he said bluntly, "since the car alone was worth forty-one the last time I checked, and he owes me five thousand cash on top of it."

It took a moment for Anna to realize that she hadn't fallen down some dark tunnel. She was still in her kitchen, still facing Gavin Marshall. Her ears were still ringing with the outrageous figure he'd quoted her.

Somewhere down the street a horn honked, setting the dog two doors down to barking. Traffic out on Northwest Sixty-third behind her back fence rumbled by, engines revving, tires squealing, radios blaring. Everything outside was normal. And the man in her kitchen claimed Ben owed him forty-five thousand dollars.

"You're not serious," she protested.

"Serious as a heart attack, darlin'. Good ol' Brother Ben is in it up to his eyeballs this time."

"Forty-five…thousand…dollars?"

"Round it off to forty-six and you've got it. Now, what was that you were saying about paying me off?"

Anna swallowed heavily. "I don't have that kind of money."

"It wouldn't matter if you did. The debt isn't yours. It's Ben's."

Finally Anna's brain clicked into gear. "What he owes you is five thousand cash. He'll bring your car back because he'll want his motorcycle. Meanwhile, you've got his motorcycle, and it's worth a considerable amount."

"True. Not enough, but considerable. But what kind of shape is my car going to be in when he's through joyriding all over the country? Every ding in the door lowers its value by about ten thousand."

"Dollars?"

"We ain't talkin' peanuts, doll."

Anna winced. He sounded like a line of bad dialogue from an old gangster movie. Not that she watched such things on television, but she'd seen bits and pieces while changing channels to something a little more intellectually stimulating.

Thinking of the amount of money Ben owed Gavin made her slightly sick to her stomach. And Gavin claimed Ben owed other people, as well.

Then a new thought occurred. There was no way she could get Ben out of this newest predicament of his unless he brought that car back to Gavin Marshall in exactly the same condition it was in when he took it. She had nowhere near enough money to pay Gavin.

I can't pay him.

Another feeling assailed her then—guilt. For she was suddenly, overwhelmingly, relieved to realize that her college money was safe. Sacrificing her savings would not begin to pay off what Ben could end up owing Gavin.

"Your brother owes me forty-six thousand dollars, and you're smiling?"

Anna swung away from him and resumed putting away her groceries. She hadn't been smiling.

Not really.

Surely not.

For supper Anna fixed herself a baked potato and small salad. She let Gavin fend for himself.

His idea of cooking was to microwave a frozen dinner.

Her plan was to pretend he was not there; to simply ignore his presence in hopes he would disappear. She was doing remarkably well at it, considering he had another baseball game blaring from the television. But when he carried his steaming plate of pasta toward her living room, she couldn't help but protest. "You're not taking that in there."

"Oh, you'd rather I join you?" Gavin smiled to himself. He didn't much like being ignored. He'd figured carrying a plate of messy pasta with marinara sauce into her pristine living room with its pale blue carpet would get a rise out of her. "Okay, sure."

He could tell by the look on her face that she'd rather he'd drop off the face of the earth. He was going to have to do something about that. He didn't much care for being disliked, either.

Then again, he didn't normally force his way into a woman's home and refuse to leave.

Well, except for that time three years ago, but that woman hadn't wanted him to leave, he remembered with a secret smile.

"You find this situation amusing?" Anna asked him tersely.

His smile stretched wider. "Let's just say I find it ironic." With a shrug, he admitted, "I'm not used to being ignored, especially by the woman I've just moved in on."

"You do this often? Move into a woman's home uninvited?"

He thought a minute, then shook his head. "No, only once. But I was invited that time, and she sure as hell wasn't trying to get rid of me my first day there. In the circles I move in, I'm actually considered quite a catch."

Anna's mouth tightened. "I'm sure."

"Hey, it's true. I'm fairly young, reasonably good-looking, rich. What's not to love?"

"If you're so rich, why don't you just go buy yourself another car and forget about my brother?"

"Are you nuts?" he demanded. "You don't just go buy another '57 Vette like it was all packaged up on a shelf just waiting to go home with you. There aren't that many of them left. That's why they're worth so much money."

She stared at him a moment, then blinked. "You mean, the car is an investment?"

Gavin studied her a moment, but couldn't read what was going on behind those eyes. "Hell, yes, it's an investment."

"Must you use such language at the dinner table?"

"Jeez, Louise, you sound as prissy as some Victorian schoolmarm."

"I assume you meant that as an insult, but I'll remind you that this is my home and you aren't welcome here. I have every right to object to objectionable language."

She laid her fork carefully on the edge of her plate. As if, Gavin thought with grim humor, it was either that, or fling it at his head. *Temper, temper.*

"If you'd told me from the beginning," she continued, "that your car was an investment, perhaps I would have understood more clearly why you're here."

Gavin shook his head in wonder. "Lady, you are just too much."

The phone rang, interrupting whatever Anna had been about to say. Surprised, because receiving a phone call was a rarity for her, she rose from the table and answered it. With a puzzled look she turned and held the receiver out toward him. "It's for you."

"I hope you don't mind." He pushed back from the table and used his napkin to wipe marinara sauce from his mouth. "I had to leave my agent a number where I could be reached."

Anna frowned. His agent?

She remembered then that he'd never answered her when she'd asked what he did for a living. Actors needed agents. So did writers and singers. He had a guitar, she remembered, so he must be a singer.

How had Ben come to get mixed up with someone who needed an agent?

She was still frowning at her uninvited houseguest when he took the receiver from her outstretched hand. They barely touched. Just a slight brushing of his fingers against hers. The hot, tingling spear that shot up her arm felt a great deal like the time she accidentally shocked herself while replacing a light switch in the den. Sharp. Startling. Her reaction was much the same as it had been then, too. She squeaked and jerked her hand away.

Anna wasn't the only one who felt the charge. Gavin felt the shock of it zap along the nerves of his hand and arm and instinctively pulled back. The receiver fell and thumped against the floor. He stared at it a moment, frowning, then bent and touched it with one finger to make sure he wouldn't get shocked again.

When nothing happened, he shrugged, chalked it up to some weird kind of static electricity, and picked up the phone. "Yeah?"

Still rubbing the side of her hand, Anna took a step back and turned away while he took his call.

"After what he did to the last one," Gavin said into the phone, "I'd as soon record it myself, and I sound like I'm gargling with sand. Turn him down." After another pause, he said, "I don't care if he's offering double that amount. That butcher's not touching another one of my songs and that's final... Bon Jovi? Him I'll do business with. The man knows what to do with a good song... Yeah, yeah, right. Let me know what happens."

He hung up the phone and turned back toward the table.

"You're a songwriter?"

Gavin somehow managed to frown and laugh at the same time. "Among other things. You make songwriting sound like it's some type of alien life form."

"I meant nothing of the sort." Well, perhaps she had, but she hadn't meant to offend him. But...a songwriter? "What type of songs do you write?"

"Rock."

"Rock?" Anna blinked in surprise.

"As in rock and roll."

"I know what you meant."

"You don't approve?"

Anna shrugged and turned back to her salad. "It's not my place to approve or disapprove. What you do with your time is your business."

"Ah," he said as he resumed his seat across from her. "But you do disapprove. I see it in your face, hear it in your voice. You don't like rock?"

"I haven't paid attention to enough of it to have formed an opinion." She did get an earful at work whenever she was in the break room the same time as Donna, but Anna deliberately tuned it out. All that screeching and hollering got on her nerves. "You said 'among other things'?"

He gave a slight shrug. "I do a little composing on the side."

"Composing? Composing of what?"

"Music." His smile was tight and strained. "I start work next month composing the soundtrack for a motion picture."

Impressed despite herself, all Anna could manage to say was, "Oh."

"I imagine you consider that a little more legitimate than rock and roll."

She bristled at his tone. "Maybe I do."

In the process of scooping up another forkful of pasta, Gavin paused and stared at her out of one eye. "Maybe I've got the wrong house. Are you sure you're Ben's sister?"

Anna gave him a terse smile. "Quite sure. Of course he played rock-and-roll music in the house when he was growing up. I didn't say I hadn't heard it, only that I haven't given it my attention. I usually have more important things to do than pay attention to—'' she'd started to say "something so trivial," but realized how insulting that would sound ''—what kind of music my brother listens to.''

"Listens to? Don't you mean plays?''

Anna shrugged. ''Plays, listens to, it still all comes out of the radio.''

Gavin's eyes widened. ''Maybe I really do have the wrong house. You don't mean to tell me you've never heard Ben play the piano.''

"Of course I have. He's very talented, especially with gospel and modern classics.''

Gavin slowly placed his fork on the edge of his plate and used his paper napkin to wipe a dab of sauce from his lip, all the while staring hard at Anna. ''You're kidding, right?''

Anna frowned. ''About what?''

"I'm beginning to think I know more about your brother than you do.''

Anna ground her molars together. ''I doubt that.''

"Then how can you mention his gospel and modern classics and not mention his rock?''

She sighed. ''I'd hoped he had quit fooling around with that by now.''

"Fooling around?'' he cried, incredulous.

"You mean, he still plays it?''

"Plays it? Ben Collins is the hottest piano player to hit the L.A. music scene in years. With a little more polish, and some work on his singing, he could give Elton John and Billy Joel a run for their money someday.''

Anna felt a sinking sensation in the pit of her stomach. ''Ben…is a professional…musician?''

"That's an even lower life form than a songwriter,

isn't it? You make it sound as if I just announced he's a professional nose-picker.''

Which was just about the truth, as far as Anna was concerned. So few people ever earned a decent living as musicians, and those who did, well, Anna shuddered thinking of the life-style of a professional musician, particularly in the field of rock and roll. Alcohol, drugs, groupies. Wild parties, destructive behavior. The thought of Ben living that way made her want to weep.

"I had hoped," she admitted, "that he would find more stable work."

"What do you mean by 'stable'?"

Anna gave him a wry smile. "Something with regular pay, company benefits, insurance, a retirement plan. I've never heard of a rock musician with a retirement plan." In truth, she'd never really heard of a rock musician who lived long enough to need one.

"Is that the kind of job you have? A stable one with all the benefits?"

Her smile lost its wryness. "There's not much that's more stable than bookkeeping."

"Ah, a bean counter."

Anna hated that term. "The last time I counted beans, I counted four of them as the doctor removed them from Ben's nose. That was a long time ago."

Gavin grinned again. "I can imagine. What was he, twenty-one at the time?"

"The doctor?"

"Ben."

"When he stuck beans up his nose? Of course not. He was four."

"It was a joke, Anna."

"Oh." Flustered, and still troubled over learning

about Ben's piano playing, Anna realized her appetite had fled. She carried her dishes to the sink, rinsed them, then placed them in the dishwasher.

Now what was she supposed to do? It was too early to go to bed, yet she had no desire to sit around making small talk with her uninvited guest for the rest of the night. She could pay a few bills. They weren't really due yet, but at least she could do it at her desk in the den. That would get her out of the living room while Gavin watched that blasted baseball game. Yet she wasn't entirely certain that she wanted to leave him on his own.

Baseball, motorcycles, old cars and rock and roll. Did the man do nothing serious? Nothing *real* or meaningful?

It seemed not. It seemed that everything he did was just for fun. No real job, no regular car, no real responsibilities.

Those were assumptions on her part, she admitted. She didn't really know the man. But so far, everything he'd said about himself led her to believe that he was one of those people who flitted through life with no cares, never contributing anything meaningful to society, never having to work hard at anything. Just out for a good time.

No wonder he knew her brother.

Ouch. What a disloyal thought.

Disloyal, but painfully true. Ben was the same way. Just out for a good time, regardless of the consequences. And there were always consequences. Anna was usually the one left to deal with them.

Realizing that she'd been wiping the same spot on the kitchen counter over and over with the dishrag, Anna rinsed the rag again, squeezed out the excess water, and hung it from the hook inside the cabinet door beneath the sink.

If she wasn't going to leave him to his own devices, what was she supposed to do? Sit and make small talk with a rock-and-roll songwriter? She knew nothing about small talk, even less about rock and roll. Should she snuggle up beside this stranger who'd invaded her home and watch a baseball game? She knew slightly more about baseball than rock and roll, but it certainly wasn't on her list of things she enjoyed watching.

And why, she wondered, was she even considering any of these ideas? This was her home. If she didn't want the television tuned to a baseball game, all she had to do was change the channel.

Feeling as if she'd just made a life-altering decision, Anna turned and marched to the television. After turning it off, she pulled the morning paper from the magazine rack beside the couch and settled down next to the lamp to read. In addition to providing her with something to read, the paper also served to block her view of Gavin where she'd left him at the table, and his view of her.

Being unable to see him did not help chase him from her mind. She knew every time he took a bite of food by the clink of his fork against the plate, every time he sipped his iced tea by the quiet thump of his glass against the table. She knew when he finished eating by the scrape of chair legs across the floor, his footsteps into the kitchen, water running in the sink. More clanks and clinks.

She knew his mother must have had some impression on him during his growing up years, for Anna distinctly heard him place his plate, silverware and glass in the dishwasher.

What she did not know was a single word of what was printed on the page she was staring at.

His footsteps crossed the kitchen floor, the dining area, then quieted against the carpet as he neared the couch. Then there was a loud *whack* and a couple of really impressive swearwords.

Anna peered around the edge of her paper to see that he'd run into her coffee table with his shin. His grimace as he bent to rub his shin shouldn't have pleased her. "Did you hurt the table?"

He grunted and limped the rest of the way to the couch. "I think it'll survive."

"I'm glad. I'm awfully fond of it."

"I'll remember that," he said with disgust. "So. I take it you don't like baseball."

Anna turned her head toward him without really looking at him and frowned as he sat at the opposite end of the couch. "Not at two hundred decibels in my living room."

"Two hundred decibels is impossible," he informed her with a small smile. "We'd be dead and the whole neighborhood would be gone."

Anna pursed her lips and turned back to her paper.

"It probably wasn't over sixty," he added.

"Thank you for correcting me."

"No problem. Mind if I read the funnies?" He slipped the back section of the newspaper from beside her and turned to the back page where the comic strips ran each day. After about thirty seconds, he let out a laugh. Then another. And another. Every few seconds he laughed.

It was irritating, that deep bass chuckle. Some people were so easily amused.

For the third time Anna started over on the lead front

page article about federal funding for the Oklahoma City Bombing Memorial.

From the other end of the couch came the crinkle of a newspaper being folded.

"So what do you do for fun around here?" Gavin asked.

Giving up on making sense of the funding article, Anna opened the newspaper to an inside page, the better to cut off her view of the man beside her. "If you're bored, Mr. Marshall, I assure you I won't be offended if you leave."

"You know," he said in a conversational tone, "in some ways your brother knows you pretty well. You did offer to pay me the cash he owes me. But in other ways, I'm about to decide he doesn't know you at all. How can that be?"

Anna turned another page, the paper rustling loudly. "I'm sure I don't know."

"I guess maybe the two of you aren't as close as I assumed, which is only natural, I guess, since you're so much older than Ben."

Turning another page, Anna crackled the paper as loudly as she could.

"Ben seems to think you're the kindest, nicest, gentlest soul on the planet. He obviously doesn't know about this prickly side of you. He thinks you're an angel. I'd have to say you're more like a porcupine."

Anna shut her eyes and slapped the pages of the newspaper together. "I can't do this."

"Is my talking disturbing you?"

"Your presence is disturbing me. You're going to have to leave, Mr. Marshall."

"My name is Gavin. My friends call me Gav."

"How nice for you. But you're still going to have to leave my house."

"As soon as your brother shows up."

"No." She shook her head and turned to look at him for the first time since he sat down. "You can't stay here. I can't allow you to stay here." She shook her head again for emphasis, her stomach tying itself in knots. "You're going to have to go stay in a motel. Or better yet, go home. If you'll leave a number, I'll let you know if Ben shows up."

He studied her a moment with narrowed eyes. "Now why," he said slowly, "don't I believe you?"

"You have to believe me." She struggled to keep the emotion from her voice. "You can't stay here."

He shook his head and smiled slightly, his blue eyes turning hard. "I meant, I don't believe you'd call me when Ben shows up. You're too used to protecting him."

There wasn't much she could say about that. He was right. It had been a desperate argument, and a lie. It shamed her, for she wasn't a liar. But her fear shamed her, too, for she had never been a coward. "How do I know you won't murder me in my sleep tonight?" she blurted. And that shamed her, too, for she wasn't a blurter.

The man on the other end of her couch had the audacity to look offended. "Murder you? Is that what you think I'm here for?"

"I'd be a fool not to consider it."

"Good God, woman, no wonder you're so prickly, if you think I'm a murderer."

"I'm a woman."

"I noticed."

"Not a very large one."

"Oh, I don't know." He gave her the once-over with those blue eyes of his. "I'd say you're just about right. Although you're not my type."

"As if I wanted to be." She stared at him a moment. "Just out of curiosity, what is your type? An empty-headed groupie who worships the ground you walk on?"

His smile came slowly and grew large. "Pretty much, yeah."

Anna's mouth tightened. She should have kept her curiosity to herself. With resolve, she returned to her previous line of thought. "Do you know how many women are murdered in their homes in this country each year?"

"Actually, no."

"Neither do I, precisely, but it's thousands. Thousands. Murdered in their own homes. By men. Men they know, or strangers. I'd say you fall a little into each of those categories. Doesn't letting you stay in my house double my chances of getting myself killed?"

"Aren't you being just a little bit paranoid?"

"I'm supposed to take a chance with my life? On the word of a stranger? I'm sorry, but taking chances is something I don't do."

"Well, now." He slid one arm along the back of the couch and watched her with narrowed eyes. "That's funny, since I consider you one of the biggest chance-takers I've ever heard of."

"That's absurd. You don't know anything about me."

"Don't I? I know you took a hell of a chance when you were eighteen and your parents died and you decided to raise your twelve-year-old brother yourself."

"That's a little different from gambling that the intruder in my house means me no harm."

"I do mean you no harm." His piercing look was a direct contrast to his words, and the easy tone in which he spoke them did nothing to ease Anna's worries.

"Oh, well," she offered sarcastically, "I guess that means I have nothing to worry about."

His jaw flexed and his lips thinned. "I agree that a woman has to be careful. But you'll have to forgive me if I seem a little testy. I've never been accused or even suspected of being a murderer before. It's not sitting real well with me."

"I can't help that."

He let out a huff of breath. "No, I suppose you can't."

"If you're as nice a person as you'd like me to think, you'd take yourself to a motel to wait for Ben."

"I guess I'm not that nice." His smile was thin and meaningless. "Okay, let me lay it out for you. I like your brother. I think he's basically a good kid who's just never been taught responsibility."

Anna's stomach twisted a little tighter at the words.

"Maybe that's your fault for always bailing him out of trouble."

The words stung like a slap across the cheek. Anna dropped her gaze to hide the pain that must surely show in her eyes.

"Maybe," Gavin continued, "it's just his nature. Either way, he's headed for real trouble if he doesn't straighten up. I don't want to see him get into real trouble. I don't think you do, either."

"You're not responsible for my brother."

Instead of answering, he just looked at her. Finally he said, "No, I'm not. And neither are you. He's responsible for himself. I'd just like to make sure he learns that lesson before it's too late."

"Why do you think teaching him is your place?"

He shrugged. "Maybe it's not. But I don't see anybody else willing to do it. Dammit, Anna, I like Ben. He's basically a good kid. He just needs to do some growing up."

"Which has nothing to do with your staying in my house," she said, a note of desperation creeping into her voice.

He huffed out a breath. "You don't have a thing in the world to fear from me."

"So you say."

"For cryin' out loud, lock your bedroom door if you're so worried about me."

"I've lived in this house since I was eight years old. Until you showed up, we've never had a reason to put locks on our bedroom doors."

"Get yourself a butcher knife from the kitchen and sleep with it next to you," he quipped. "I saw a baseball bat in Ben's closet. Take that to bed with you. Drag one of those dining room chairs in there and prop it under your doorknob so I can't get in."

Surprise held Anna quiet a moment. She could do all those things easily. Why hadn't she thought of them herself? Still, she shouldn't have to barricade herself in her own bedroom. She opened her mouth to say so, but he beat her to it.

"I'm not leaving. If that bothers you, I apologize. But I came here to teach Ben a lesson, and that's what I'm going to do, whether you like it or not."

She felt like a fool, but a safe one. Her sharpest butcher knife was tucked beneath her pillow, Ben's old

Louisville Slugger stood beside the bed, and the back of a dining room chair was snugged up beneath the doorknob to prevent anyone from entering. That should do it.

If she had to go to the bathroom in the middle of the night, she'd probably kill herself trying to leave her room. But no one was going to come in without waking her in the process, and if they made it in, she would not be helpless.

Sitting on the edge of the bed in her knee-length nightgown, Anna admitted to herself that she thought the chances of Gavin Marshall trying to murder or molest her were zero to none. His plans for Ben, and the look in his eyes when he spoke of them, worried her for Ben's sake, but she felt no personal threat from the man.

But she'd have felt like a complete idiot if she'd blindly trusted a stranger to stay in her house and she'd been wrong about him. If she'd awakened dead in the morning, she would have had no one to blame but herself for being stupid.

So she'd done the smart thing. The safe thing. No matter how stupid it felt.

It never occurred to her as she finally fell asleep around midnight that her safety precautions would be her downfall, but that was because she wasn't particularly aware of her habit of slipping one arm beneath her pillow while she slept.

Chapter Five

It was the prick of cold steel along her forearm that woke her. Confused, she moved her arm to a more comfortable position, only to feel a sharper sting along the outer edge of her hand. She might have gone back to sleep, but as the pain dawned on her, so did the sudden smear of moisture she felt on her hand.

The knife. She'd cut her hand on the butcher knife. Of all the stupid things.

Realizing that she was probably bleeding all over her sheets, Anna groaned. Bracing her other hand and knee against the mattress, she went to push herself up and off the bed, but instead of soft mattress, her knee came down solidly on something hard. She let out a small cry and jerked back before realizing the something hard was the baseball bat she'd brought to bed. At her movement, it rolled off the mattress and onto the floor, leaving her feeling like a total idiot.

The feeling was magnified when she swung her legs off the bed and stubbed her toe on the bat where it lay on the floor. And even more so a moment later when she limped toward the door, only to ram her shin into the chair that braced her doorknob to keep out the stranger in her brother's bed. She grunted in pain, then, furious, wrestled the chair out of her way and jerked open the door.

Gavin couldn't sleep. His conscience kept teasing him with discomfort, like a small sliver just beneath the skin. He should have thought of some way to get through to Ben other than by barging in on the kid's sister. He hadn't come here to scare Anna Collins.

Hell, he couldn't blame her a bit for being leery of him. He was a stranger, after all, and she was right, a woman couldn't be too careful.

Still, the thought that he might hurt her was ludicrous.

Yeah, but she doesn't know that, buddy.

No fooling.

Tomorrow he needed to find some way to make this up to her. What that way might be, he had no idea. He needed to figure out if there was something he could do for her. Something she maybe wanted that he could give her to make up for invading her home, scaring her, inconveniencing her. She was too damn prickly to open up to him, so he'd have to find some other way to ferret out what she might need or want that he could give her.

At the sudden noise coming from beyond his closed bedroom door, Gavin stiffened. After a moment he relaxed with a grin and wondered how long it had taken her to remember about the chair she'd braced beneath her doorknob. From the muffled curse, she didn't seem all that pleased with her safety precautions.

Ha! And she told me to watch my language.

Finally he heard her go into the bathroom, heard the slight click of the light switch, then the rush of water through the pipes and into the sink.

The water ran for a long time, then a drawer opened, a cabinet door closed. And the water kept running.

Frowning, Gavin sat up in bed. She was sure taking a long time. What the devil was she doing in there? He was tempted to get up and find out, but told himself it was none of his business. Probably woman stuff. She wouldn't appreciate his concern.

When he heard a soft growl of irritation mixed with pain, he tossed the covers aside and stepped into his jeans.

She'd left the bathroom door open, so he had no trouble seeing her. And what a sight, with her short hair mussed enough to look like a man had just run his fingers through it over and over. The sudden urge to run his own fingers through that short, honey-colored hair shocked him. As did the sudden rush of blood through his veins when he realized that her knee-length nightgown was so thin he could see through it to the mole on her right hind cheek. Without thought, he stepped quietly to her side.

The sight of her blood flowing bright red from an inch-long slice in her right arm just below her elbow, and a smaller cut on the outer edge of her right hand, cooled him off quicker than a bucket of ice water in the face. The blood trailed down her pale skin and turned pink where it mixed with water in the sink. Gavin swore.

At the sound of his voice, Anna shrieked and jerked,

banging the back of her hand against the faucet. "Damn." She squeezed her eyes shut for a long moment before opening them and glaring at him in the mirror. "I was right. You came here to kill me."

"What happened?"

"You wouldn't believe me if I told you. You and your stupid suggestions," she muttered.

Gavin scowled. "My suggestions? Good grief, you mean— I meant for you to put the knife somewhere close so you could get to it, not cuddle up with the damn thing. Let me see that arm."

Anna covered the cut with her free hand. "I can handle it."

Gavin snorted. "You can't even get out of bed without hurting yourself."

"This, from a man who can't negotiate his way around a coffee table?"

"Yeah, yeah, I was a charm school dropout. Stick your arm under the faucet. Where do you keep your peroxide?"

"I said," she managed through gritted teeth, "I can handle it."

"Then handle it," he answered tersely, "before you bleed to death."

"It's not very deep," she said, looking down at her arm. "It's just messy."

"Messy is right." Gavin opened the cabinet door next to the mirror above the sink and grabbed a washcloth and the brown plastic bottle of peroxide. "I can't believe you actually went to bed with a butcher knife." Setting the bottle and cloth beside the sink, he carefully pulled her arm from beneath the running water. "That is what you did, isn't it?"

"I plead the Fifth. What are you doing?" She tried to tug her arm from his grasp.

Gavin kept his hold as gentle as possible, but firm enough to hang on. "I was beginning to wonder about that."

"About what?"

He poured peroxide first into the cut on her arm, then the one on her hand. "If you had a sense of humor. Glad to see you do." He pressed the folded washcloth over the slash on her arm and placed her hand over it. "Hold that. Press hard."

"I'm sure I don't have the slightest idea what you're talking about."

"It will stop the bleeding."

She scowled at him in the mirror. "My sense of humor?"

Gavin stared at her reflection, wondering why she should suddenly seem so much more appealing to him at two in the morning with her face scrubbed clean, a little puffy from sleep, her hair mussed, than she had in the light of day with makeup on and her hair neatly combed.

Hell, he thought, returning her scowl. He'd meant what he'd told her earlier in the evening—she damn sure wasn't his type. He must still be half-asleep himself if he was thinking about leaning down and kissing that tip-tilted nose.

With a shake of his head, he pulled his gaze from her face in the mirror and looked down at her arm. "I meant the pressure on the cut. Pressure will stop the bleeding."

"I know that." Irritation, and maybe pain, roughened her voice.

Gavin grabbed another washcloth from the cabinet

to press against the smaller cut. He reached for her hand, and felt again that sharp zap of electricity. He jerked his hand away. "Stop doing that," he ordered tersely.

Anna had felt it, too, that tingling charge that had shocked her when they'd both reached for the phone. "Me? I'm not doing it. It just happens."

That, Gavin thought, was what he'd been afraid she would say. Damn, that's all he needed. A static charge every time they touched. It wasn't sexual, he told himself firmly. It couldn't be. No way.

But she couldn't cover both cuts herself, so he reached for her hand again. Sort of snuck up on it.

This time there was no shock. Relieved, he pressed the cloth against the cut. Which essentially left him holding her hand.

When was the last time he'd held a woman's hand? He couldn't remember. High school, maybe, he thought, surprised.

His fingers rested against the inside of her wrist where the skin was so transparent he could see her veins. Beneath his touch the steady beat of her pulse sped up. "Does it hurt?"

Anna scowled harder. "Some." But that wasn't her immediate problem. Her immediate problem was a sudden breathlessness, a catch in her throat. Maybe she'd lost more blood than she realized, if simply looking at him in the mirror made her feel light-headed. She looked down instead.

The change of view didn't help. She must have lost a lot of blood. Otherwise the sight of his big, dark hand wrapped around her smaller, paler one wouldn't send her heart up into her throat to flutter like a trapped butterfly.

With fingers that suddenly trembled, she lifted the washcloth from the cut on her arm. The bleeding had slowed to a slight ooze. "Uh, thanks. I can take it from here."

Gavin eased the washcloth away from the cut on her hand. "Much better." But instead of stepping back to give her room, he reached into the cabinet again and pulled out a box of strip bandages. Without comment, he poured more peroxide on her cuts, then tore open a bandage and placed it over the cut on her arm. It took two to cover it.

Anna stood still and watched him as though she weren't involved in the process at all. The fingertips of his left hand were callused, but his touch was gentle. Being taken care of this way felt odd. Anna wasn't used to anyone fussing over her. She was the one who normally did the fussing.

How many times had she cleaned and bandaged Ben's countless cuts and scrapes in his younger days? Too many to remember.

Nor could she remember the last time anyone had cleaned and bandaged anything of hers. It made her feel weak, helpless. Made her knees watery. She didn't much like it.

"Are you about finished?" she demanded.

"Aw, shucks, darlin', and here I was hoping for a big ol' kiss by way of thanks."

Anna scowled, certain this must be another one of his jokes, but she failed to see the humor. "You'll have to settle for my verbal thanks."

"That'll do fine." He finished bandaging the cut on her hand. "So? Where is it?"

"Where is what?"

"Your verbal thanks."

She gave him a tight smile. "Thank you."

With laughter in his eyes, he gave her a mocking nod. "You're welcome, Ms. Collins."

On her way out the door, Anna tossed a look past him over her shoulder before pausing to look at him. "By the way, when not in use, the seat and the lid go down. Good night, Mr. Marshall."

When Gavin woke the next morning, the sun was well up and he was alone in the house. How he knew the latter without even crawling out of bed, he had no idea. There was just this empty feeling in the air.

The idea that he could feel such a thing irritated him. It was only his imagination. He sure as hell wasn't so tuned in to Anna Collins that he could tell from behind his closed bedroom door that she wasn't even in the house. The very idea was ludicrous. And scary.

She was a quiet person. She was probably sitting on the couch reading the Sunday paper. Or at the table, eating breakfast.

The thought of food lured him from the bed. Looking down at himself, he figured he'd better at least tug on his jeans before leaving his room. In case he was wrong and he wasn't alone in the house.

The instant he opened the door a moment later, jeans in place, he knew his first waking thought had been correct. Except for him, the house was empty. There was an absence of something. Energy? Scent?

Neither idea made any sense. Anna wasn't a particularly energetic woman. She didn't fidget, didn't rush around. In fact, he hadn't noticed that she wasted a single motion, no matter what she was doing.

And how could he miss her scent when the only thing about her he'd smelled was the clean fragrance of her sleep-warmed hair and skin last night when he'd stood next to her in the bathroom? He didn't remember smelling any perfume.

So how could "something" be missing from the air? How could the air feel empty? He didn't know. He only knew, without checking, that Anna Collins had left the house.

That's bull hockey.

He of course couldn't know any such thing. He stalked into the living room to prove himself wrong.

She wasn't there. Nor was she in the kitchen, bedroom, or bath. Her car, when he thought to look, was not in the garage.

Okay, it was Sunday. She had probably gone to church.

Gavin assumed that being able to feel her absence this way was a bad sign. He had friends who spoke of being so close, so connected to a woman that they knew her thoughts, felt her feelings, sensed when she was near and when she wasn't.

That was fine and dandy for his friends, but Gavin had no desire, no intention whatsoever, of being that connected with a woman. At least not in the foreseeable future. Particularly not with a settling-down kind of woman like Anna Collins.

He didn't need that type of connection with a woman, didn't want one. Wouldn't have it. He had things to do, places to go, songs to write. No time for a regular woman of his own. He liked to keep things loose. Liked to be able to walk away whenever he wanted without worrying about leaving a broken heart behind.

Still, there was no reason to keep on making Anna

angry. While she was gone he needed to come up with an idea or two to get on her good side.

Sitting in the pew at church, Anna prayed fervently that Gavin Marshall would be gone from her house when she got home.

She'd been taught in Sunday school as a young child that God answers every prayer. What she'd had to learn on her own was that sometimes God's answer to a prayer was no. Anna was reminded of this when she pulled in her driveway and noticed that the Sunday paper, which she'd left on the porch, was gone, and that the living room drapes, which she'd left closed, were open.

This time, realizing that Gavin was still there, God's answer didn't feel like a simple no. It felt like a "No, and furthermore, Anna, my dear..."

Sitting in her car staring blankly at the garage door, Anna took a slow, deep breath. Maybe if she were nicer to Gavin, she could get him to tell her what Ben had been up to lately. Maybe if she made friends with him she could get him to leave. It seemed worth a try. Nothing else was working right in regard to that man.

Resigned to trying to be nice to him—although to be honest, he was rather likable in a rough sort of way—she got out of her car and went to open the garage door. She didn't waste her time praying that the door would open easily for a change. Instead she used her key to open the lock, then bent, grabbed the handle, braced herself, and pulled hard, putting her back into it the way she knew she had to, to get the door to budge.

Instead of hanging, dragging and groaning in protest, the wide, heavy door flew up in its tracks so fast that

Anna barely got her hand free of the handle before being yanked off her feet. A sharp squawk of surprise escaped her throat. She lost her balance and staggered against the brick wall beside the door.

Immediately she straightened and glanced around to see if any of her neighbors was looking.

Then, feeling silly for checking, she looked up at the garage door, wondering what had happened. Cautiously she reached up to pull the door down to try it again, just to see what would happen. It was surprisingly harder to pull down than usual. Normally, one tug and the double-wide door more or less fell down its tracks and slammed closed and woe be to anyone standing in the way. This time she had to actually tug it—although only slightly—all the way down.

It couldn't be broken. Please, God, it couldn't be broken. She had no money set aside for a new garage door.

With more reluctance than care, Anna bent and grabbed the handle again, this time pulling gently. The door raised easily. Easier than she ever remembered. It rolled up all the way without much effort on her part at all. Slowly she turned in a circle, craning her neck as she looked up at the door where it rested in its tracks above her head.

The door to the kitchen opened and Gavin smiled at her. "What do you think?"

Frowning, Anna looked back up at the garage door. "Is it broken?"

Gavin laughed. "It's fixed."

Anna straightened and stared at him. "Fixed?"

"Try it again."

She did. Again it went down at a controlled speed instead of a crash. And again, it flew up with virtually no effort. Amazed, she closed and opened it yet another time.

Gavin got a kick out of the look on her face. As if she'd just discovered ice cream for the first time in her life. "Like it?"

Actually, he got a kick out of looking at *her*. He couldn't remember the last time he'd seen a grown woman looking so damn prim and proper. Her pink suit was more feminine than tailored, with a waist-length, collarless jacket. The skirt hit the bottom of her knees, and her white blouse sported a crisp wide bow beneath her chin.

Prim. That was the only word for it, for her. Except maybe for cute.

Slowly, Anna smiled. She didn't want to smile at this man, but she and that stubborn, heavy garage door had hated each other for years. "What did you do?"

"Adjusted the tension."

"That can't be as simple as you make it sound."

He gave a slight shrug. "Pretty simple. It only took a few minutes."

Anna pursed her lips to hide her smile. "You disappoint me. You'd have been better off to tell me you'd spent hours fixing it and that you broke three fingers in the process. Just so I could feel properly grateful."

There came that sense of humor again, Gavin thought. The one Ben said she didn't have.

But as Gavin looked into her eyes, he realized there was no humor there, the smile was forced.

Damn. She wasn't joking. "Is that what Ben would have done?"

Anna turned abruptly away and marched toward her car. "Thank you for fixing the door."

"I'm sorry," he said quietly but loud enough for her to hear. "None of my business."

Anna opened her car door, then turned to face him with another fake smile. "Don't apologize. I appreciate your efforts. That door and I have been enemies for years."

The prim pink Sunday suit was gone, and Gavin found himself missing it. Which was absurd.

After pulling her car into the garage and making another fuss over the garage door, she'd gone to her room and changed clothes. The suit had been replaced with beige slacks, tailored white blouse tucked in at the waist, brown leather belt, white socks and white sneakers. Everything straight and neat, as though she had to pass inspection. Instead of prim, now she looked too damn neat for comfort.

It occurred to him that she never looked as if she were comfortable. She always looked stiff, on guard. Did his presence cause that, or was she just an overly cautious woman? Or overly uptight?

Not his problem, he told himself. Except that if he was the cause, it was his problem.

And that hint of a bandage showing through her sleeve, not to mention the bandage on her hand—those were his doing.

Dammit, he hadn't come here to scare or upset her or cause her any trouble, yet he'd done all three. He was sorry for that. But not sorry enough to give up and let her brother off the hook.

He sat on the couch and watched as she went to the kitchen, listened as she rattled around in there for a minute. The fridge opened. Ice cubes clinked. Liquid poured. Then she surprised him by returning to the living room and taking the chair across from the couch, a sweating glass of iced tea held in both hands.

"What do you do with yourself on a Sunday afternoon?" he asked, keeping his voice easy.

His question took her by surprise. She took a slow sip of tea. "What do you mean?"

He flopped against the back of the couch and accidentally kicked the coffee table while crossing one foot on the opposite knee. He frowned at the table that always seemed to be in his way. Then he shrugged. "I mean, do you go visit friends? Cook out on the patio? Go to the zoo? Fly a kite in the park? What do you do?"

She couldn't help it. She laughed. "Me? Fly a kite?" The idea was ludicrous.

"You don't fly kites?"

She tilted her head and studied him. "Do you?"

"I've been known to."

"Why?"

He blinked. "What do you mean, why?"

"Why does a grown man fly a kite?"

"For fun."

She frowned. "Fun?"

Something in the back of Gavin's neck tingled. "Enjoyment? Entertainment? You know—fun."

She gave him a look that seemed to say, *If you say so.* "I wanted to talk to you about Ben."

"I'd rather talk about fun. What do you do for fun?"

"Mr. Marshall—"

"If you don't start calling me Gavin, I'm going to have to get rough with you."

To give her credit, she didn't look impressed with his threat. "How long have you known Ben?"

Gavin studied her through narrowed eyes. "That depends on who you're asking."

"Pardon?"

"If you're asking Mr. Marshall, that's my dad. He's known Ben for several months."

Her foot started a rapid tapping on the carpet. "All right. "How long have you known my brother, Gavin?"

Gavin grinned. "A little over a year."

"Why did you lend him money?"

His smile slipped. "If he wants you to know, he'll tell you himself."

She shook her head. "I'm not asking why he borrowed it from you."

The words were hard for her to say. Gavin could read every thought that crossed her face. He could feel the sudden tension radiating from her, feel it pulling at him. She might not be asking why Ben borrowed the money, but she damn sure wanted to know. Or thought she did.

"I'd like to know," she continued, "why you would bother lending him the money at all."

Trevor shrugged. "He's a friend. If I hadn't loaned it to him, he'd have gotten it somewhere else that maybe wasn't too smart."

She seemed to shrink in on herself. "You mean, like a loan shark?"

"A thumb-breaker? Yeah. It was a possibility." There were other possibilities, worse ones that made his gut clench thinking of them, but he didn't mention them.

"So you loaned him the money yourself."

"That's right."

"Because you're such a nice guy?"

"Why, thank you."

"I was asking a question, not stating an opinion."

Gavin placed a hand over his heart. "You wound me."

Her mouth firmed, lips thinned. The lady obviously was not amused. "When and how did you meet my brother?"

He gave a negligent shrug. "At a party."

"What kind of party?" she asked sharply.

"You've been reading too many tabloids, sugar."

"What kind of party?"

He shrugged again. "Just a get-together at a friend's. Ben was pecking out a tune on the piano. Something, I learned later, that he'd written himself."

"Ben wrote a song?" There was that baby-owl blink again.

"He's written several in the past year."

She cocked her head. "You like him."

"Yeah. I like him. I've told you that several times. He's a likable guy."

Deep furrows dug into her brow. "If you really like him, then why…"

"Why am I after his hide?"

"Is that what you're after? His hide?"

Gavin shook his head. "I'm not out to hurt him, Anna. But I think if he doesn't wake up real quick, he's headed for trouble. Bad trouble. I like him too much to sit back and let that happen without trying to stop it."

She took a small sip of tea and stared down at her glass for a long moment before looking up at him again. "I don't understand what it is you're planning to do if and when he shows up here. I don't understand what you think you can do."

"I can make him own up to his responsibilities."

"How? By telling him to? Do you think I haven't tried that?" Her voice wavered. "Do you think I don't know his faults?"

"I don't know," Gavin said bluntly. "Do you?"

From the neighbor's backyard, a dog barked. Out in the street, a car door slammed. Ordinary sounds of an ordinary neighborhood. They soothed something in Gavin, eased the tension that tightened his shoulders whenever he thought of the trouble Ben was headed for if somebody didn't give him a hard, swift kick in the seat of his pants.

"Are you aware," he asked her quietly, "that he likes to gamble? And that he's not very good at it?"

He read the pain in her face before she spoke. "He promised me he wouldn't do that again."

"You sound just like my aunt Marilyn." Gavin's wry laugh was tinged with sadness. "The two of you have a lot in common. Or rather, her son, Danny, and Ben have a lot in common. Unfortunately."

Anna took another sip of tea, pursed her lips and leaned back in her chair. "I suppose you're going to explain what you mean."

Gavin sighed. "I suppose I am. Marilyn is my mother's sister. Her three boys were in their early teens when her husband left her. Danny was the youngest. About twelve, I guess, when his dad ran off."

Gavin hadn't been much older himself at the time. Lord, he'd never forget the day Marilyn and the boys had come crashing into the house, awash in hysterical tears. Steve had left them. Just said goodbye and waltzed out the door.

Gavin shook his head. It was a long time ago now. "The two older boys, Steve Junior, and Tom, they did okay with it after a while. But Danny apparently couldn't accept that his dad was never coming back. He started acting up, getting in trouble in school, that sort of thing.''

Ah, the look on Anna's face was priceless. She knew where he was headed with this story. He could read it in her eyes. She was already tallying up the similarities between Danny and Ben. Ben's parents might not have walked out on him deliberately, but dying was still leaving, and the ones left behind still felt anger and pain and a sense of betrayal.

''The older Danny got,'' Gavin continued, ''the more trouble he managed to stir up. By the time he was twenty, he'd milked nearly ten thousand dollars out of his mother to get him out of one scrape after another. The rest of us kept telling her to stop, but she couldn't. He was her baby. She loved him. She couldn't just stand back and do nothing when he needed her.''

Pain and stubborn denial mixed with fear in Anna's eyes. Gavin wished...hell, he didn't know what he wished. Only maybe that she wouldn't hurt so much, wouldn't care so much. But Ben was her brother. If she didn't care, Gavin wouldn't admire her—and he was starting to realize that he did—he wouldn't be feeling this dull ache in his chest on her behalf.

''She sold her new Lincoln and bought an old clunker, she hocked her jewelry, mortgaged her house. And good ol' Danny just kept coming back asking for more. She borrowed every cent she could from anyone who'd lend it to her, until finally she couldn't borrow any more.''

''It's a sad story,'' Anna said, denial hard on her face. ''But it has nothing to do with Ben.''

"Doesn't it?"

"No. I've never gone into debt for Ben." But only because she couldn't, Anna acknowledged silently. She'd been too busy paying off the debts their parents had left them.

"Good for you. Marilyn wasn't that smart. If she had cut him off sooner, maybe he wouldn't have ended up where he did."

Anna did not want to hear the rest of this story. She most definitely did not. "I suppose you're going to tell me where he ended up?"

Gavin gave her a single nod. "I am. When his mother couldn't lend—give—him any more money, he tried the rest of the family. Everybody told him to grow up, to stop being so damn irresponsible. Danny didn't listen. He kept throwing his money away, kept gambling, kept losing. Eventually he lost too much to the wrong kind of people. The kind who break kneecaps for fun. My brother bailed him out of that one after making Danny promise to straighten up and get counseling, get a job."

"But he didn't."

"No, he didn't." It still hurt, Gavin thought. After two years, it still hurt to think about what Danny had done, where he was now. "He turned right around six months later and got in even deeper with the same people. Only this time no one was willing to bail him out. So he came up with another way to get the money he needed. Unfortunately, he wasn't very good at that, either. He's now a guest of the State of Washington, doing twelve years hard time for armed robbery."

Anna shivered and looked down at the glass of tea she still held, mildly surprised to notice that her knuckles were white and the glass was in danger of shattering. She eased her grip.

Not Ben. Ben wouldn't end up like Gavin's cousin. Ben wouldn't——

"Right about now I figure you're telling yourself that couldn't happen to your brother."

Anna flinched but refused to look up.

"Don't kid yourself," he said. "It can happen. Probably will, if he doesn't straighten up. One of these days he'll be in so much trouble you won't be able to bail him out. Then what will you do?"

This time she did look up at him. "So I stop helping him now? Speed up the process so he can get in real trouble that much sooner? What kind of answer is that?"

"If we handle it right, maybe he'll learn his lesson now, before it's too late."

"We?"

"You and me, Anna. Together. What do you say?"

"I say that considering what you do for a living, it's incredibly presumptuous of you to think you can teach responsibility to anyone."

His eyes hardened. His voice softened. Dangerously, she thought.

"What I do for a living?"

"You write songs, Gavin. Rock-and-roll songs. If that's not a frivolous and irresponsible way for a grown man to spend his time, I don't know what is."

Chapter Six

So she thought his work was frivolous, did she? An
irresponsible waste of time. Not nearly as earth-
shattering a profession as bookkeeping.

It stung. More than it should. Gavin hadn't had to
put up with snide remarks about his chosen profession
in years. Maybe he was getting soft.

But then, in the circles he generally moved in, no
one was likely to consider rock a frivolous pursuit.
Nearly everyone he hung with was in the business.
Why should he care what Anna Collins thought?

But he did care, and there was the rub. And he didn't
know what, if anything, to do about it, or if there was
anything he could do. Yet he felt things when he
looked at her, things he wasn't sure he'd ever felt before. Things he couldn't—wouldn't—identify. He
wanted her to like him.

Damn. There it was. He wanted Anna's approval, of

what he wanted to teach Ben, and of himself. He wanted her to approve of Gavin Marshall. And she didn't.

If the rest of Sunday was any indication, she didn't want anything to do with him. After she'd snapped at him she'd closed herself up in her room for hours. When she finally came out, she didn't speak a word to him all evening.

All right, it was Monday and she was gone to work. To her responsible, important job.

"Her boring job," he said out loud to himself. Dull, predictable, rule-ridden.

Comfortable in nothing but jeans, his hair still damp from the shower, Gavin roamed through Anna's home, room by room, looking for clues to the woman who somehow intrigued him.

It worried him a little the way she filled his thoughts when she wasn't even around. He told himself that the only reasons he couldn't get her off his mind was that he was in her house, surrounded by reminders of her, and that she was so closely tied in with his determination to straighten out Ben. It was not, he assured himself, because he was attracted to her, because he wasn't. No way. Not him, not to a stay-at-home, no-nonsense woman like her.

Even her home was no-nonsense, he thought as he wandered through it. He deliberately avoided her bedroom, figuring he'd already invaded enough of her privacy as it was. But he felt no qualms about wandering the rest of the house.

There was a great deal to be learned from the knick-knacks and collectibles that filled a person's home. In Anna's case, there was a great deal to be learned by the lack of them. Even in her decorating, if it could be called that, Anna Collins was a no-nonsense woman, plain in every way, no frills, no extra touches to deliberately brighten up the place. Yet everything was painfully neat. Not a single thing out of place, unless Gavin himself had left it there.

No houseplants, not even fake ones.

No photographs of their parents. None of Anna. Just a graduation shot of Ben in cap and gown, grinning like a goofball. Typical high school picture. Nice-looking kid. The framed photograph was the only adornment to the stark white walls of the living room.

The third bedroom had been converted into a combination den-office-music room, with a worn brown sofa along one wall and a small desk in the corner. Centered beneath the window on the outside wall sat an old blond upright piano, a metronome, still and silent, sitting on one corner.

Grinning, Gavin had a sudden picture of Ben grimacing over scales and exercises, just waiting for the chance when no one was listening so he could cut loose with a little boogie-woogie. And Anna, rushing in, frowning fiercely, reminding him he was supposed to be practicing, not playing. *A piano is not a toy.*

He could almost hear the echo of her voice. It made him smile. So stern. So practical. So serious. Always serious.

Looking at the piano, Gavin wondered if she'd ever played it. Then he shook his head. Not her. She was too practical for something as frivolous as music, at least when it came to her own time, her own enjoyment.

What Anna Collins needed, Gavin decided, was to lighten up, have some fun. Learn how to enjoy life.

And he was just the man to teach her.

He would start her off with a pleasant surprise.

It was more than a surprise, it was a shock, when Anna stepped in from the garage Monday evening and was met with the mouthwatering aroma of home-cooked meat loaf. For a moment she thought she'd entered the wrong house. No one but Anna had cooked in this kitchen since she'd taken over the chore from her mother at the age of twelve.

"Welcome home." Barefoot, wearing faded jeans and a Rolling Stones T-shirt, Gavin executed a grin and a quick little bow.

Anna glanced around the kitchen, saw the mess of cooking—empty bowls, utensils, a spill of something red on the counter. Across the room, the table was set for two. Beside her, the oven radiated heat. "You cooked?"

He beamed like a little boy bringing a fistful of dandelions to his mother. "I cooked."

She didn't want to be charmed, but couldn't seem to help it. This was the last thing she'd expected from him. Not only that he could, but that he would put himself to the trouble. It made her slightly uneasy. She wasn't used to people doing things for her. Especially strangers. Especially after the way she'd insulted him yesterday.

Then she felt herself flush. She'd asked about him at work today. Donna, who worked at the desk next to Anna's and handled payroll and accounts receivable, was always listening to rock in the break room, always ribbing Anna for her disinterest, her lack of knowledge on the subject.

Today Anna had surprised her by asking if she knew anything about rock-and-roll songwriters. Donna had been curious that Anna would ask, but no, she'd said, popping her gum, she'd never heard of Gavin Marshall. "Unless he's that gorgeous hunk on the Grammies last year, the one whose songs always win awards."

Now Anna wondered, was this the same man? What would a Grammy-winning songwriter be doing making meat loaf in her kitchen?

"By the time you change clothes, dinner will be on the table."

"Do you mind if I ask a question?" Startled that the words had come out of her mouth when she'd sworn they wouldn't, Anna kept her gaze firmly on her plate and used her napkin to blot her lips. The question she wanted to ask had been haunting her since yesterday when he'd told her about his cousin Danny. It had plagued her sleep, and distracted her all day today at work. She couldn't get it out of her mind.

"Ask away," he offered.

To give herself time to arrange the words properly, she took another bite of the excellent meat loaf. "Where did you learn how to cook?"

"From my mother."

"It's very good." Anna took another bite in hope that as she swallowed the food, the question on her tongue would go down with it. "Excellent in fact."

"Thank you. Mom will be pleased to know you approve and that I haven't forgotten everything she taught me. Is that what you wanted to ask me about? My cooking?"

She felt her face heat up. "No. No, it isn't." Still stalling, she sipped her tea, added another dab of margarine to her mashed potatoes. Stirred her peas with her fork. "It's about your cousin. Danny."

Gavin eased back in his chair and looked at her. "What do you want to know?"

She didn't want to ask, but knew she was going to anyway. She was compelled. She just didn't know how to word the question. "It's about Danny and his mother."

"What about them?"

She took a deep breath for courage. "Did he like her, dislike her? Did he respect her? Disrespect her?"

Gavin cocked his head and frowned slightly.

"I guess I'm assuming he couldn't have thought much of her," Anna said, "since he took advantage of her, used her the way he did."

Gavin shook his head and cut into his meat loaf. "If that's what you're assuming, then you'd be wrong. And I'll answer the question you're really asking." His voice softened. So did his eyes. "Your brother worships you."

Her face flamed again. "That's not—"

"To him, there isn't anything in the world you can't do. He thinks you're the greatest. He knows he could have ended up in foster care when your parents died, but you managed to keep him with you. He knows you worked your tail off to pay the bills and see that he finished high school. He loves you, Anna."

"Then why?" she whispered, her voice breaking despite her will. "Why does he keep using me the way he does? Why does he only come home when he wants money? Why does he keep breaking his promises to me?"

With the first tear that slipped down her cheek, Gavin was out of his chair and kneeling beside her, wrapping his arms around her. "He doesn't do it to hurt you, Anna, he doesn't. He just takes you for granted, that's all. He assumes you'll always be there for him. Don't cry, honey. Come on, you're killing me here.''

She sniffed, wiped a hand across her eyes and pushed away from him. "I'm not crying."

He gave her a crooked smile and used his thumb to catch a final tear. "Good."

She sniffed twice more. "I never cry."

"Never?"

"Never. It's useless."

"I hear it relieves tension, makes you feel better."

"It stops up your nose, makes your eyes red and gives you a headache. A waste of time."

She'd obviously found her balance again, so Gavin backed off. It was surprisingly hard to do. He resumed his seat.

"I owe you an apology," she said quietly.

Gavin smiled. "You didn't get me that wet."

"I mean for what I said yesterday, about your song-writing."

"Forget it," he said with a wave of his fork.

"I can't. It was unforgivably rude of me. I'm normally overly polite, I'm told."

"I guess I just bring out the best in you. Forget it. You said what was on your mind."

"No." She shook her head, squared her shoulders, met his gaze steadily. "I was angry that you thought Ben could end up like your cousin. Angry," she said, her voice falling, shaking, her gaze dropping to her plate, "because I'm afraid you're right and I don't know what to do about it."

Gavin let out a slow breath. This was the first time she'd admitted Ben was heading for serious trouble.

She raised her gaze to him again. "I took it out on

you, and I'm sorry. I don't know anything about rock-and-roll music or what it takes to write a song. I'm sure that what you do brings enjoyment to a lot of people."

"I hope it does." He wished one of those people who found pleasure in his work was her. "But you still find it frivolous."

She gave him a weak smile. "I find most things frivolous unless they have to do with day-to-day survival." She winced. "Ouch. That sounded…pathetic. I didn't mean it that way."

"It sounded scary as hell," Gavin said. "Life is short, Anna. Everyone's entitled to a little enjoyment now and then. It helps make the bad times less bad. I've been trying to find out what you do for enjoyment."

With a determined smile, she picked up her fork. "I eat meals cooked by someone else. This really is delicious." So delicious, in fact, that she decided not to say anything about the damp towel in the bathroom floor, the toilet seat he'd left up, the whiskers in the sink and the two pairs of shoes in the living room instead of his room where they belonged. "Honestly, it's wonderful."

"Come on, you can do better than that. What do you do for fun?"

She shrugged, took a bite of meat loaf. "Read. Watch television."

"Now we're getting somewhere. What do you like to read?"

"You know, the usual. Biographies, self-help books, that sort of thing."

Gavin nearly choked on a swallow of iced tea. When

he stopped coughing several moments later, he stared at her. "*That's* your idea of fun and enjoyment?"

Her expression sang of hurt feelings. "What's wrong with it?"

"Oh, darlin', we're going to have to do something about you."

Anna was positive that she did not care for his tone, nor the amusement twinkling in his eyes.

To redirect his thinking, she asked, "When did you say Ben left to come here?"

Gavin's smile faded slowly. "Sometime before noon Wednesday."

"Then where is he?" she asked, worry creeping through her. "You said he was coming here. He should have been here by now."

Gavin frowned at his plate. "Maybe I was wrong. The note he left said he was going to get the money he owed me. Since he always comes to you when he needs money... Don't take offense. He's admitted that to me several times."

"He promised me last year that he would never ask me for money again. Maybe he's trying to keep that promise."

"By going somewhere else for the money?"

"Where would he go?" But Anna feared she knew the answer.

"Somewhere he could place a bet and hope to win. Let's see if we can find him." Gavin pushed back from the table and stood.

"What are you going to do?"

"Go to the fount of all information these days—the Internet."

From his duffel bag Gavin took his notebook computer and connected it to Anna's phone jack by the desk in the den.

"I don't see how you're going to find Ben this way."

"You'd be surprised what you can find out on the Net. The world is a much, much smaller place than any of us realize. There's a musicians' newsgroup that should be able to help us track him down."

He reset his dial-up settings to use his service provider's 800 number instead of the local Santa Monica number he normally used, then logged on to the Internet. From there he went one at a time to three of the newsgroups he frequented and posted messages for anyone who had seen Ben during the last few days to e-mail Gavin.

"Now what?" Anna asked.

"Now we wait and see if someone responds. It might be a day or two before we get anything, but if Ben hits any of the usual places, somebody on one of those newsgroups will spot him and let me know."

It didn't take a day or two for information. When Gavin checked his e-mail an hour later he had a message from an old friend in Las Vegas who had seen Ben the night before, winning at the craps table in one of the casinos.

Frowning, Gavin e-mailed back that if his friend saw Ben again, tell him Gavin was looking for him.

"Las Vegas," Anna said, her eyes filled with distress.

For that look in Anna's eyes, Gavin could cheerfully strangle Ben Collins.

Tuesday evening when Anna came home from work Gavin had another surprise for her. One living room chair had been moved aside to make room for a full-blown stereo system with so many buttons and lights it was dizzying. Plastic bags, cardboard boxes and large sections of packing material littered the floor, coffee table, chairs.

"What have you done?" she demanded, her blood chilling at the thought of what a setup like this must cost. Not to mention the mess.

"Damn. Either you're early, or I'm running behind."

"I'm not early. What have you done? Where did all this come from?"

"Then I'm late. I meant to be finished before you got home." He grinned up at her from where he knelt in front of the three-foot-tall speakers.

"I would hope so." Eyes wide, Anna surveyed the damage to her once-neat living room. "Look at the mess," she cried.

He blinked and looked around. "What mess?" He frowned at the scattered packaging. "That? Oh. I'll take care of it."

"You most certainly will. When you box everything up and take it back where you got it."

Tilting his head, he peered at her through narrowed eyes. "Now why would I want to take it back?"

"Because I'm not paying for it."

His eyes widened. "Of course you're not. Who asked you to?"

Anna forced a deep breath, but said nothing.

"Look again, darlin'." His voice took on an edge. "I'm not Ben. I didn't spend your money or charge anything to your account. Frankly, I'm insulted that you'd think I would."

Realizing her mistake, Anna felt her cheeks sting

with heat. It had seemed so normal to come home and find a man had brought a new toy into her house and expected her to pay for it. But he was right. He wasn't Ben. He wasn't her father.

"I'm sorry," she told him. Then she thought to ask, "How did you get all this here on that motorcycle?"

He pursed his lips, took a slow, deep breath, then relaxed. "I had it delivered. Now, you have to go out and come back in."

Anna blinked. "I beg your pardon?"

With a screwdriver in his hand, he gestured toward the back door. "Go back out, count to ten—make it twenty. Twenty-five. Then come back in."

"What are you doing? What is all this stuff? You can't possibly get this mess cleaned up in a count of twenty-five. I'd have to count to five hundred. Twice. Slowly."

"Oh, ye of little faith. A little trust, please. Just go out for a minute, then come back in."

"I'm already in. I see no point in going out again, only to come right back in."

"The point," he said, putting down his screwdriver and rising to grip her shoulders and turn her toward the back door, "is in the fun."

She skidded to a halt on the kitchen floor and peered skeptically over her shoulder at him. "Fun?"

"Fun. It's not a four-letter word. Go." He gave her a nudge toward the door. "And don't forget to count."

An amazing thing happened as Anna stood in her broiling hot garage and counted slowly to twenty-five. A sense of what could only be called anticipation bubbled to life in her chest. She knew that she was considered, by all who knew her, to be a dull, humorless person. The thought never fazed her. She was also thought of as smart, honest to a fault and highly responsible. Those things, in her opinion, were much more important.

Ben, when he came home on his infrequent visits, was always trying to get her to go out with him to a nightclub or an action-adventure movie or a rock concert. Stick-in-the-mud. That's what he called her.

Wastrel. Irresponsible. That's what she'd tried so hard not to think of him.

She couldn't help it if she'd never learned how to have fun. When other girls her age were playing hopscotch on the sidewalk, Anna had been looking after her baby brother while her parents were out partying, or at home sleeping off the last party. She'd understood even then that other families worked differently, but she'd never let it bother her.

The thought of her parents made her head ache. She had such ambiguous feelings about them. She had loved them, worshiped them, but she had never been blind to their faults.

They had loved her and Ben, but they had been so young themselves—their mother had been sixteen when Anna was born; their father, seventeen. They never finished growing up. Love, to them, did not necessarily equate with responsibility. By the time Anna was ten, she was virtually in charge of the house and her baby brother. Mama and Daddy had been more than likely to forget they even had jobs—when they'd had them—or bills to pay, much less children.

There was always a party to go to, a new toy or gadget to buy, a trip to take. A bet to place.

That was where Ben came by his love of gambling. Both their mother and father had been gamblers. Not very good ones, but they had loved it. It was all a game to them; life, children. Just a game.

If Anna wanted clean clothes, she learned early to wash and iron them herself. If once in a while she'd wished she could go out and draw squares on the driveway and hop around on one foot with the other girls instead of cleaning the house or cooking supper, she got over it. She had never had time for such games, never learned the appeal of them.

But Gavin Marshall somehow managed to make the prospect of having fun seem…fun.

What would it hurt to let down her guard and see how the rest of the world lived? If she managed to make a fool of herself in front of him, so what? He was only temporary in her life. He would be gone soon and she would never see him again.

So, against what she considered her nature, she stood in the suffocating garage and counted. When she reached fifty, she decided it was too hot in the garage for fun. She opened the door to the kitchen and breathed a sigh of relief as air-conditioned air hit her like a welcome wall of ice.

"Okay, I went out. Now what—" She stopped abruptly at the edge of the living room, amazed. Every scrap of debris, every plastic wrap, every cardboard box, was right where it had been, scattered across the room. "I thought you were going to clean up the mess."

"What mess? Here." He took her by the arm and led her toward the couch. "Sit right there."

"You want me to sit on the cardboard box or the plastic bag?"

"See? I knew you had a sense of humor." He

JANIS REAMS HUDSON 111

shoved the packing materials onto the floor. "How's that?"

With her purse still hanging from the crook of her arm, Anna planted her hands on her hips. "You're going to clean up every bit of this."

"What?" He glanced around the room, but his mind was obviously on something else. "You mean, the boxes and stuff? Sure. No problem. But first, sit."

"I cannot possibly sit surrounded by this much trash."

Gavin heaved a sigh and rolled his eyes. "You're bound and determined to ruin this, aren't you?"

"I don't even know what *this* is. But cleaning up this mess can't possibly ruin anything. It might send the garbagemen to the chiropractor, but at least the room will be livable."

"Okay, okay." Grumbling about how some people had no sense of adventure, Gavin tore through the room, stuffing bags, cardboard and thousands of little white peanuts into the boxes the equipment had come in, carting the boxes to the garage.

With an extra pair of hands, Anna decided, the work would go twice as fast. Besides, how could she trust him to get it all when he hadn't even noticed it was there? She started gathering some of the trash herself.

Gavin practically barked at her. "Sit. I said I'd do it, and I will."

Dammit, he'd wanted to surprise her, and she wasn't cooperating. She was more concerned with a little debris than with him or the equipment he'd brought into her home.

Imagine thinking she would have to pay for it. It added another dimension to the picture he had of how things went around here when Ben showed his irresponsible face.

Gavin picked up the last box, gave the room a final sweep, and carried the box to the garage.

"All right, that's done. Ah, hell. Go change clothes. You can't do this all trussed up in a suit."

"Do what? Precisely?"

He grinned. "Nothing illegal. Just... Will you just go change clothes, please?"

By the time she came back, the pizza he'd ordered had arrived and Gavin had found his good mood again. "Much better," he lied. She was still trussed up, this time in pressed slacks, button-down shirt, socks and sneakers. Repressed, he thought yet again. "Now sit. Eat."

She picked up the pizza box from the coffee table and headed for the dinette.

"Oh, no." He snatched the box from her hands. "Just get napkins and something to drink. Plates, if you insist."

"You don't mean for us to eat in the living room."

"That's exactly what I mean." The struggle on her face was interesting. Poor girl was so uptight and set in her ways, she couldn't even imagine breaking her routine enough to eat pizza in the living room. "Come on," he encouraged, wiggling his brows. "Live dangerously."

She looked down at the pale blue living room carpet, then seemed to come to a decision—a difficult one—before looking up at him. "You'll be careful? You won't spill anything?"

With a hand to his chest, he gave her his best wounded look. "What do I look like, a slob?"

She pursed her lips.

"Never mind. Don't answer that. I'll be careful, I promise. It's carpet, Anna, not hammered gold. Just get the napkins and drinks, will you?"

With a look of reluctance, she finally turned toward the kitchen.

Gavin knelt beside the new stereo system and dug the stack of CDs out of the Blockbuster bag. He took his time, trying to let go of his irritation that had reared again. He didn't want to be ticked off when he introduced her to rock and roll.

He could have avoided all the trouble and expense—not that he would miss the money; hell, he was rolling in it these days—by just having her watch MTV.

Nah, too far out for a novice to appreciate. Too scary if he'd had her watch late at night when they aired the really weird stuff.

VH-1, then. He could have gone with that. They played a lot of good stuff. But he wanted to introduce Anna to the music without the distraction of visuals. Visuals that could prejudice her against the music, he thought, picturing some of the videos he'd seen lately. Some called them art. Anna, he feared, would not. So he had decided on CDs. Pop, mostly. Middle-of-the-road, mainstream stuff. It seemed the best place to start.

Anna returned with plates, napkins, two glasses of iced tea and two lap trays. She wasn't taking any chances, he thought, with her pale blue carpet.

He found the CD he wanted, plucked it from its case and slid it into the unit. "All you have to do is listen. With an open mind, if you please. No judgment, no prejudice allowed."

"You still haven't told me what's going on."

"Music Appreciation 101. Introduction to Rock and Roll."

Her expression shifted from suspicious to deadpan. "You're joking, right? You know I don't always get jokes."

"No joke." He adjusted the volume so as not to shatter her eardrums, then crossed to where she still stood. With a light touch to her shoulders, he nudged her until she sat on the couch. "Lesson number one. This," he said, plopping down next to her and reaching for his tray, "is Sting."

Music pumped out of the three-foot-tall speakers with a strong beat and wailing guitars.

Watching Anna was an experience. She reached for a slice of pizza and stared at the speakers across the room, her concentration on the music total. She probably didn't know that she blinked in time with the beat.

"All right, I think I've got it." It was after ten and Anna's brow was still furrowed in concentration.

"What do you mean, you've got it?" She was taking her intro to rock so seriously, Gavin didn't know whether to laugh or pull his hair out.

"Sting, Bon Jovi, Aerosmith, Bruce Springsteen." She ticked off her fingers. "Billy Joel, Huey Lewis, Bryan Adams, Elton John and what was that last one? Oh, yes. The Rolling Stones."

Gavin shook his head and rolled his eyes. "I was hoping you would enjoy the music, not just memorize the names of the artists."

"But I did enjoy it," she claimed, brows arching.

She looked and sounded sincere, but she hadn't relaxed once all night, hadn't tapped her toe in time to the music, hadn't smiled. "Coulda fooled me," he muttered.

"No, seriously," she protested. "Some I liked better than others, but—"

"Which ones?" He thought he'd catch her lying, just trying to make him feel as though he hadn't wasted his time. And his money.

"Well, Sting has the smoothest voice, Springsteen the most raw, most elemental. I like the piano, so Billy Joel and Elton John appealed to me. Some of Bon Jovi's songs were nearly as hard-driving as the Rolling Stones', but I think I prefer Bon Jovi's ballads. As for Aerosmith and Huey Lewis—"

"Okay, okay." Laughing, Gavin held up both hands in surrender. Impressed despite himself, he shook his head. "You're right. You've got it. You pass with flying colors. Even if I don't think you really enjoyed it."

She cocked her head. "Why do you think that?"

"Because you looked so serious."

Slowly Anna straightened her shoulders. "Wait a minute. Were any of those songs yours? Did you write them? Was I supposed to, I don't know, yell and scream or something?"

"No." He laughed. "I didn't write any of those songs, and no, you weren't supposed to yell and scream."

She shrugged. "I enjoyed listening to everything you played."

If what he'd witnessed tonight was her idea of enjoyment, well, hell. Maybe the woman had no soul.

But Gavin wasn't ready to give up. If music could soothe the savage beast—or whatever—surely he could find the right music to get a genuine reaction—a positive one—out of Anna Collins.

Music blared out of the radio as Gavin's '57 Corvette raced across the Golden Gate Bridge into San

Francisco. Ben Collins tapped his fingers against the steering wheel in time with the music. No doubt about it, the car was a honey.

He threw his head back and laughed. The look on Gav's face when Ben had driven off had been priceless. Honey, indeed. Ol' Gav had looked as if Ben had been making off with his best girl.

Ben had a feeling that Gav wasn't going to be too happy with him when he got back. Gav was a good guy, but sometimes he acted more like an older brother, or a father, than a buddy, carrying on about one thing or another.

But hey, he'd left him the key to the Harley, hadn't he? It wasn't as if he'd left Gav stranded.

Ben knew that Gav liked to carry on about his getting his act together, getting a job, staying away from the cards and the dice. Okay, so maybe Gav had a point. Ben was thinking on it. Meanwhile, L.A. had gotten a little hot when he'd bet a thousand dollars that he didn't have on a card game, and lost.

He hadn't been able to bring himself to go to Gavin for more money; he already owed him five grand. But Skinner wasn't known for his patience. He'd vowed to take the thousand out of Ben's hide if he didn't pay up.

Since he couldn't pay up, and since Skinner had put the word out and no one in town would take his bet these days, Ben decided it was time for a little vacation of the out-of-town variety, preferably not on the Harley they'd be looking for him to be driving.

He had hit Las Vegas and made back the thousand he owed Skinner within an hour. If he had just stopped then and gone back to L.A. and paid Skinner, everything would have been fine. But how was a guy supposed to stop when he had a cool grand in his hand just begging to be gambled?

He had turned that grand into three, then lost it. Then he'd spotted a friend of Gavin's on the strip.

"Ladies and gentlemen," he murmured with a wry grin, "Ben Collins has left the city."

San Francisco had always been good to him. He would win the money back, then go home and pay off Skinner and Gavin. Who knew? He might even think about getting a job.

Wouldn't Anna be surprised if he did?

He could have gone to her for the thousand. What the hell else did she have to do with her money, anyway? She would have gotten that sad look in her eyes that always made him feel lower than a slug, but she would have given him the money.

But he had promised her he wouldn't ask her for money anymore. He wanted to keep that promise. She deserved that much from him, at least.

"Be good to me, San Francisco."

Chapter Seven

"Bon Jovi."

Donna Weeks stopped chomping her gum in midpop and gave Anna a quick double take. "What?"

"That song you're humming. Bon Jovi, third cut on their 'Destination Anywhere' CD."

"Well knock me over with a feather." It was Wednesday morning, and the offices of the accounting firm of Smith, Smith, and Bernstein were quiet, with just Anna and Donna in the accounting office. Both grinning at each other. Which was odd all on its own, because Anna Collins was not a grinner. Now she was not only grinning, but admitting to recognizing a rock-and-roll song?

"And here I thought you never listened when I play the radio in the break room."

Anna chuckled, and she wasn't a chuckler. But it felt good to have something other than work in common with the woman she'd sat beside for three years. Good, and warm. "You could say I've had a crash course lately."

And she wondered secretly what surprise Gavin Marshall might have waiting for her that evening when she went home from work.

Oldies. Gavin's Wednesday surprise was Top 40 hits from the fifties and sixties. These Anna remembered from her childhood, because her parents had listened to oldies. But she began to understand that Gavin was waiting for something from her, some reaction to the music he selected. Because she wasn't sure what that something was, she was unwilling to give him any but the mildest reaction, so she kept her knowledge of this music to herself, merely stating that she enjoyed listening to Buddy Holly, Elvis, Chuck Berry, the Platters, Nat King Cole, Dion, the Drifters.

"So?" Gavin eyed her skeptically. "What do you think?"

Anna ran what she'd heard during the past few hours through her bookkeeper's brain, compared it to what she'd heard the night before. Her eyes narrowed in thought. "Considering the advancement in technology after these recordings were made, they're surprisingly good, technically speaking."

"How about musically speaking?"

"Not as hard-edged as some of the rock from last night," she offered, "but some of it, like Elvis and Buddy Holly, are more—earthy, I guess you'd say. And overall, the lyrics of the oldies are more innocent, more fun."

As Anna said good-night, Gavin shook his head and flopped back against the couch. The music wasn't reaching her. She was too focused on analyzing it, comparing it, tallying the results as though she'd listened to a string of numbers rather than songs.

A few minutes later, before turning in for the night, Gavin checked his e-mail and learned that a friend of a friend thought he'd seen Ben in San Francisco, but wasn't certain. If he found out for sure, he would let Gavin know.

Thursday night Gavin tried country music on Anna. Garth Brooks, Reba McEntire, Brooks and Dunn, Alan Jackson, Trisha Yearwood, Vince Gill, Toby Keith. This time he at least got a smile out of her with songs like "Friends in Low Places." A smile, but that was it. Again she analyzed, tallied and reported faithfully on what she'd heard.

Now he was really beginning to wonder if the woman had a soul.

Saving classical music as a last resort, because he knew the least about it, Gavin waited for her to come home from work Friday, wondering if the Broadway show tunes he'd selected would reach something inside her. Even if they were mostly the movie soundtracks instead of the stage production versions.

He started her off with a few of the more famous numbers from *Oklahoma!*, *Showboat* and *The Music Man*.

"Progress," he muttered when she laughed out loud at a young Ron Howard's rendition of "Gary, Indiana" from *The Music Man*.

But it was while she listened to the original cast recording of *The Phantom of the Opera* that Gavin first got a hint that something new was happening inside Anna.

During the instrumental version of the title song, near the beginning of the two-CD set, she started sitting up straighter. When "Angel of Music" hit its full-bodied stride, Anna slowly pulled away from the back of the couch. When Christine and Phantom sang the title song, Anna's breath came faster.

Gavin felt his own pulse begin to race in response to Anna's reaction to the music.

Then "Masquerade" filled the room with its vibrant, swirling power, and Anna scooted to the edge of the couch. "Oh, my." Her eyes widened as she held out her arms and stared at the gooseflesh that had risen there. She looked at Gavin with glowing eyes. "This is what you've wanted me to feel?"

She may have been tuned in to the music, but Gavin was tuned in to her. The excitement, the *life* in her eyes, the way her pulse fluttered at the base of her throat, her struggle to keep air in her lungs... Damned if he wasn't getting turned on just watching what the music did to her.

It was as though he'd been seeing her through a film that had just been swept away. Or fog, now blown away by the wind.

This, he thought, was the real Anna Collins.

They sat that way, facing each other, Gavin staring at her in awe, Anna staring blankly at him, until the final echos of "Music of the Night" in Michael Crawford's powerful voice faded at the end of the final CD, leaving the room vibrating with silence but for the sound of Anna's breath catching in her throat.

"Such...power," Anna whispered, dazed by it. "Such emotion."

"It's excellent music," Gavin managed.

Slowly Anna shook her head. "I don't mean the music, exactly. I mean what I feel, inside, when I hear it.''

Gavin's pulse thumped. Damn, if she didn't stop looking at him like that he was going to have to kiss her. And the way he was feeling just then, it wouldn't stop there. "What do you feel?" he managed.

She tilted her head back and closed her eyes, baring her throat to him in a gesture that struck him as erotic. The look on her face was that of a woman being joyfully filled by a man while making love.

Sweat beaded along Gavin's spine.

"I feel…stirred. Moved. Powerful. Breathless.'' Her pale, exposed throat worked on a swallow.

Gavin found himself swallowing with her.

Then she straightened and opened her eyes, looked away. "You probably think I'm being foolish."

"No." His voice rasped, as if he hadn't used it in days. "No, I don't.''

"Is this what you feel when you listen to rock and roll?''

One corner of his mouth curved up. "Not usually, no.'' What she felt, what he was feeling just then, was something he doubted he'd ever felt, even during sex.

Someday, he vowed, he would make love with Anna Collins with that music that had stirred her soul washing over them.

Better yet, he wanted to be the one to put that look in her eyes, that hitch in her breath. To stir her soul, the way watching her for the past hour had stirred his. No phantom between them when they made love. Only the two of them and the passion.

The pleasure, the power of it, would likely kill them both.

* * *

It wasn't so much the music that followed Anna into sleep that night as the look in Gavin's eyes when, gazes locked, they had listened through the end of the CD. Even knowing that there was no new word on Ben through Gavin's e-mail failed to chase Gavin's look from her mind. He had looked, she thought, as if he could have eaten her alive.

When she woke Saturday morning, the memory of it shook her, more so than had the actual event.

At the time, she had been wrapped up in the music and he had been part of it. But the music was gone now, only a faint whisper left in the back of her mind. The look in Gavin's eyes, the husky timbre of his voice, still stirred something deep inside her. Something hot. Exciting. Forbidden.

Lust.

Good grief. She sprang up in bed, her eyes wide, her heart pounding. She, Anna Lee Collins, was in lust.

It struck her then, the irony of it all. She had felt more last night, was feeling more right now, than she had the one and only time she'd had sex. In sheer delight, she laughed out loud.

What had it been—four years, five—since that highly forgettable experience with a man who'd come and gone from her life almost as fast as she'd wished he had? Any sense of anticipation that had led up to that interminably long thirty minutes had been lost in nerves.

Yet now, just remembering the look in Gavin's eyes had anticipation sizzling through her blood. Who would have thought that blue could be so hot?

Not that there was a thing in the world she would do about it. Her laugh this time was self-directed. There was no way that a big-time rock-and-roll songwriter from California would be even remotely interested in a mousy bookkeeper from Oklahoma. He was temporary in her life, here only because of Ben.

But still, Anna was suddenly glad Gavin Marshall had come into her life, no matter how temporary, no matter the reason. She liked him.

The thought surprised her. She genuinely liked him. If she felt more than that, well, that would just be her little secret. There was no need to embarrass them both by letting it show.

"So what's on your agenda for today?"

Anna had her head beneath the kitchen sink, her rear in the air, fishing out her rubber gloves when Gavin's voice came from directly behind her. Startled, she gave a small cry and instinctively raised her head. Right into the underside of the sink. "Ouch!"

"Bet that hurt."

"You scared me. I didn't hear you coming."

"Sorry." He flashed a grin. "So, what are you doing?"

"Getting ready to clean house."

"Didn't you just do that the other day?"

"Last Saturday."

"Ah." He nodded. "You're one of those."

"One of those what?"

"One of those people who sets herself a schedule and sticks to it week after week, year after year."

"And your point?"

"Reminds me of my mother. Cleans the house every week right on time whether it needs it or not."

Anna tugged on a rubber glove and smiled. "Believe me, after a week of you, the house definitely needs cleaning. Your poor mother. I imagine that while you were growing up, the house needed cleaning every *day*. It sure does now," she muttered.

"Hey," he protested good-naturedly with a hand to his chest. "I resemble that remark."

"Yes." She smirked. "You certainly do. What is that saying? If you're not part of the solution, you're part of the problem?"

"Ouch. I'll just, uh, stay out of your way, then."

"Good idea, unless you want to be dusted and vacuumed."

She pulled on the other glove, grabbed a handful of cleaning rags from the bottom drawer, and gathered her cleaning supplies from beneath the sink. On her way out of the room, she paused and looked back at him. "Gavin?"

"Yeah?"

"Thank you for the music."

His smile warmed her to her heels. *"Phantom?"*

"All of it. I can't remember when I've spent a more enjoyable week," she said softly. "Thank you."

"My pleasure."

The way he said it in that deep, gravelly voice of his made her almost believe it was. With her pulse beating just a little too fast, she hurried into the bathroom and attacked the tub with its week's worth of soap film and hard water deposits.

During the course of cleaning the bathroom, she heard Gavin go into his room and shut the door. He came out a few minutes later, then the kitchen door opened and closed. She didn't think anything of it until she'd cleaned her way back to the kitchen thirty minutes later and realized he had never come back into the house. She was just about to step outside and look for him when she heard the outside water whining through the pipes.

Frowning, she opened the door to the garage.

She should have guessed. The big door was up, and Gavin, wearing nothing more than a ratty pair of denim cutoffs, was washing the motorcycle in the driveway. It was hard to decide which to shade her eyes from, the blinding reflection of sunlight off chrome, or the breath-stealing display of bare skin stretched over flexing male muscles. Mercy. Ben never looked like that in his cutoffs.

That's not your brother you're drooling over, Anna girl.

And she was drooling, metaphorically speaking. The instant she realized it, she stepped back into the kitchen and slammed the door. Good grief, her heart was pounding. Just from looking at him.

Yes, but there was so very much of him on display for you to look at. All that skin, bronzed by the sun. All those muscles, strong and toned. That dark patch of hair on his chest. And all of it sparkling with a sheen of sweat and a fine mist of water from the hose.

The only thing Anna could think was, *Wow.*

Gavin heard the back door slam and looked up, but there was no one there. Disappointment surprised him. The hope that Anna would come outside and talk to him surprised him. Neither should have. Constantly in his mind, Anna was.

The sound of footsteps behind him on the driveway had him turning, hoping somehow that it was her, even though he knew it couldn't be.

The girl coming up the drive in sprayed-on biking shorts, an equally tight and revealing top that ended several inches above her navel, looked to be about seventeen. One ear sported three small silver stars, with a slice of a quarter moon dangling from the other. When she walked, she bounced, back arched so he'd be sure to notice that there was plenty of her to bounce.

He knew the type. Jailbait. Bored and looking for trouble.

"Like, hi." Her eyes gleamed like a hungry predator spotting its next meal.

"Morning."

"You must be a friend of Ben's."

Gavin's lips quirked. "Must I?"

"Don't mind me, I'm, like, just another nosy neighbor in a neighborhood full of, like, nosy neighbors." She grinned and stuck out a hand bearing four gaudy rings that surely would turn her fingers green any minute. "I'm Sissy Roberts, from across the street."

Gavin shook hands. "Pleased to meet you, Sissy Roberts. Gavin Marshall."

"I figured you for a friend of Ben's. I mean, that's his Harley, right? And anyway, you wouldn't be here to see Anna."

Gavin arched a brow. "I wouldn't?"

"Nah, nobody comes to see her. She keeps pretty much to herself, never goes anywhere. Dullest lady on the block. So how'd you end up with Ben's Harley? Hey, he didn't, like, sell it to you or something, did he? My daddy's always told him if he, like, ever decided to sell, he'd, like, buy it. Boy, Daddy's gonna be, like, mad."

"No need," Gavin said, tucking her comments about Anna into the back of his mind. "We, like, swapped vehicles for a while."

The girl dug the toe of one sneaker into the concrete

and swayed back and forth. "I can't imagine Ben letting anybody, like, touch his Harley."

Gavin grinned. "You think I stole it?"

Cocking her head and sticking out her rather sizable chest, she studied him. "You don't look like a thief," she said, trying for sexy with her voice and doing a credible job of it.

"What does a thief look like?"

"You know, like on TV, like, scuzzy. You're, like, not scuzzy at all."

"Gee, like thanks." Spotting a fleck of tar he'd missed on the rear wheel, Gavin pulled a rag from his hip pocket and reached for the bottle of tar remover.

"So, like, is Ben coming home soon? I mean, to get his Harley or anything?"

"I expect he'll be along anyday now."

"Well, you tell him Sissy from across the street said hi."

Like hell I will. But Gavin glanced up and nodded. "I'll be sure and do that."

As he watched her bounce that ripe little body back across the street, he shook his head. If Ben Collins got within twenty feet of that piece of trouble looking to happen, Gavin would break his legs. Surely even Ben wasn't that dumb.

After cleaning the bathroom and changing the sheets on her bed and Gavin's, Anna dusted and vacuumed her way through the house. When she hit the den and turned to straighten the items on the desk, something was off. Missing.

Her car keys. She always left them beside her purse.

She wasn't worried, just curious. After all, no one had been in the house but her and Gavin.

Her questions were answered a moment later when she stepped out the front door. Hot, heavy air hit her like a wall and pressed the air back into her lungs as she tried to exhale. Gavin had finished with the motorcycle and had parked it on the grass beneath the maple tree that shaded the front lawn. He had then backed her car out of the garage, where he now stood hosing it off. The play of muscles across his back threatened to steal what little air she had left.

"You don't have to do that," she said, approaching him from behind.

At the sound of her voice Gavin turned his head to look over his shoulder and smile. "Do what?" His movement shifted his aim just enough to angle the spray toward the outside mirror. From there it ricocheted straight into the side of his head. He ducked, squeezed his eyes shut. His mouth dropped open in shock as he released the nozzle trigger to cut off the spray. Water plastered one side of his hair against his skull and streamed down his face, off his nose and chin.

Anna couldn't help it. A snicker came first, but when he opened one eye and glared at her, she broke out laughing.

Something long empty inside Gavin, a hole he hadn't know existed, filled with warmth and light at the sound of her laughter. It was the first time he'd heard her laugh, but he vowed it wouldn't be the last. If he had to play the clown to accomplish that, so be it.

But a devil took over just then. "You think that's funny?"

Anna saw the maniacal gleam in his eye and started backing up, holding one hand out in front of her.

"No," she sputtered between bursts of laughter. "No, it's not—" She struggled for breath, to stop laughing, and failed on both counts. "Not a bit."

"Uh-huh." For every step she took backward, he followed. "Let's see how funny you think this is." He let her have it in the chest.

Shocked that he would spray her, and that the water was so cold, Anna shrieked and sucked in a sharp breath. "Oh!"

Gavin hooted with laughter.

"Oh!" Her eyes were wide with shock as she used a thumb and forefinger to pluck the soaked fabric of her shirt away from her skin. "I can't believe you did that!"

"No?" His laughter turned, to her ears, sinister. "Wanna see me do it again?" He raised the nozzle and aimed.

"No!" Laughing now, because she couldn't seem to help herself, Anna backed farther up the sidewalk.

Gavin got her again, this time in the stomach. She stumbled back, tripped over a crack in the sidewalk, and abruptly found herself sitting in the flower bed, a clump of purple petunias on either side of her and one, she was certain, squashed beneath her. Her fingers sank knuckle-deep in damp earth.

"Oh, yuck!"

Gavin laughed so hard he had trouble standing.

Anna pulled her hands from the muck and shook them. It didn't help. "Look at me," she complained, laughter still in her voice. She raised her gaze slowly to him. "I believe I'll have to get even for this."

"Ah, but I'm the one with the hose," he taunted.

"In fact," she said as if he hadn't spoken, "I'm sure

that if you look up the phrase 'getting even' in the dictionary you'll find my picture.''

Smiling, and carefully aiming the hose away, Gavin stood over her. "Will it help if I apologize?"

"Are you any good at groveling?"

"I don't know. I never tried it." He chuckled then at her mock glare and sobered appropriately. "If you'll hold your arms out I'll wash off the dirt."

She narrowed her eyes. "I'm supposed to trust you?"

"Certainly." But his grin said, *If you dare*.

"Hmm. I question your sincerity, but since I don't want to take all this dirt and mud back into my clean house, I guess I'll have to trust you."

His grin widened. "Atta girl." He crimped the hose and took off the spray nozzle so he could have a nice even stream that wouldn't spray out. Unless he wanted it to.

Anna held her arms out, and held her breath, fully expecting to get squirted in the face.

But Gavin Marshall was good at keeping her off balance. She was on her rear in the flower bed, wasn't she? He leaned down and wrapped an arm around her waist, lifting her from the flower bed. He ran a gentle stream of water over one hand, using his free hand to help dislodge the dirt.

The water was cold; his hand, and his eyes, were hot. Anna shivered. And wondered what it would feel like to have his hand move up her arm all the way, then down to cover her breast.

Shocked not only by her body's heated response to the thought, but stunned that the idea had even occurred to her, she opened her eyes, only just then realizing that she'd closed them.

He released her hand and took up the other one, treating it to the same startlingly sensual rinsing. He was looking at her. Watching her. Reading her thoughts, it seemed to her. She flushed, embarrassed to her core that he might know what she was thinking.

He did know. She read it in his eyes as heat flared there, and an answering heat flared deep inside of her.

Then he blinked and lowered his gaze to her hand. "There you go."

The playful tone in his voice eased the tension inside her. She chuckled in relief. "I find myself wanting to say thank you, out of habit. But since it was your fault I got muddy, I don't think I will."

"My fault," he protested in mock innocence. "All I did was spray you with water. You found the mud all by yourself."

Anna pursed her lips. "I'm beginning to develop a real sympathy for your mother."

"What's that supposed to mean?" he asked, eyes narrowed in playful suspicion.

"It means, that if she's got even half her wits about her after raising you, she deserves a medal of honor."

"I still have the hose."

"I'm going in now." She spun quickly toward the house. "Thank you for washing my car."

"Hey, Anna," he called when she reached the front porch.

She paused and looked back over her shoulder. "What?"

"I missed a spot."

"Where?"

"Right—" he pointed the nozzle he'd just replaced, and squeezed the trigger. A hard jet spray hit her in the rear.

Chapter Eight

"You should have seen the look on your face."

Three hours later, and Gavin was still bragging about getting the drop on her with the hose.

To his benefit, he was doing a credible job of making up for soaking her. He had insisted on taking her out to dinner, someplace nearby, casual, because all he'd brought on his trip were jeans, plus he didn't want her to go to the trouble of dressing up. They had settled on the all-you-care-to-eat buffet at Catfish Cabin.

It was a family restaurant, informal, with friendly waitstaff. The smell of fried catfish hung on the air not unpleasantly. Anna knew she wouldn't—couldn't—eat enough food to justify the cost of the meal, but the restaurant was losing money on Gavin, so she calculated that it evened out all right.

"Your eyes must have been as big around as silver

dollars. I'll bet you gaped about like this catfish did when he got himself caught for dinner.''

Anna took another bite of the tender, steamy fish and savored the delicate flavor. ''You know, it's really going to feel good getting even with you. I never could get revenge on Ben when we were kids. He loved to do the typical boy things, you know, like a frog in my shoe. Not unlike spraying an unsuspecting person with a garden hose. I believe he was ten the last time he pulled that one.''

Gavin grinned over his corn-on-the-cob. ''Is that your way of telling me I was childish?''

''I wouldn't dream of saying such a thing.''

Oh, but Gavin loved that sparkle of laughter in her eyes. ''If you could never get even with Ben, what makes you think you can with me?''

''Because you're not six years younger than me and you can't get me in trouble with our parents for picking on a little kid.''

''Ah, the old 'Mama, she's picking on me' routine. Know it well.''

''I'll bet you do.''

''Were your parents musical?''

Anna blinked. ''Pardon?''

''What part didn't you understand? Parents, or musical?''

''Funny. The question threw me, that's all. No, they weren't musical, unless you count the radio, or their old stereo.''

''I just wondered how Ben came to be so damn good on the piano.''

Anna smiled. ''He is good, isn't he? But it certainly wasn't inherited. He came by it via threats and bribes.''

''Come again?''

She took her time spreading butter on a hot, yeasty dinner roll. "By the time he was twelve, Ben decided he was through with the piano. Mama had started him on lessons, but after she and Daddy died, he was, after all, the man of the house. He couldn't be bothered with piano lessons."

"I was a twelve-year-old boy once. Their egos are so damn fragile. So you threatened and bribed?"

"I tried logic first."

Gavin chuckled. "I bet that went over well. To the average twelve-year-old boy, there is absolutely nothing logical, or even sane, about piano lessons."

"You do know him, don't you?" she asked with sour humor. "I very calmly explained to him that I was working two jobs to keep him out of foster care, keep a roof over our heads and food on the table."

Ben had told Gavin some of this, but he'd glossed over it. Now Gavin was getting a clearer picture of what Anna had gone through to take over raising her kid brother after their parents were killed. She hadn't had an easy time of it, despite the lighthearted way she described the things she'd had to do.

"I cooked all his meals, washed—not to mention paid for—all of his clothes. I asked only that he mow the yard in the summer, keep passing grades at school and be home by nine on weeknights. I didn't think practicing the piano thirty minutes a day was too much to add to the list."

Gavin grinned. "You've obviously never been a twelve-year-old boy, or you would have known better."

"True enough. But there was one thing Ben wanted more than anything in the world, and that was Daddy's Harley."

"That's right, he told me it had been his dad's."
Gavin let out a low whistle. "He must have made practicing the piano into a religion to get his hands on that bike."

Anna chuckled. "Not quite. We had to cut a deal. He played the piano every day for thirty minutes, unless he was deathly ill, or I would sell the Harley to Mr. Roberts across the street."

"Ah, that would be Sissy's father."

Anna's eyebrows inched up her forehead. "What have you been doing? Making the rounds of the neighborhood while I'm at work all day?"

"She bounced—I mean, walked over and, ah, introduced herself while I was washing the Harley this morning."

Anna made a choking sound and covered her mouth with her napkin.

"What, no comment? And she had such nice things to say about you."

"I'll just bet she did. She and her friends egged my house last year at Halloween."

Gavin winced, thinking of peeling paint and disgusting window screens. The smell of rotten eggs if the goo wasn't washed off before the sun dried it. The flies. He'd done his share of egging in his misspent youth.

"She's not one of my favorite people," Anna added.

"Can't say as I blame you. Anyway, threatening to sell the Harley must have done the trick. He's good, Anna. Really good."

She smiled with pride. "I know."

"So," he said as casually as possible, "when he finally left the nest, why didn't you get married and raise kids of your own?"

"Oh, and after doing such a fine job with Ben, right?"

"He was twelve years old, his personality more than set by the time you took over."

"But I didn't help much, did I? I never made him stand on his own."

"So maybe you'll do things differently when it's your own children."

"In case you haven't noticed," she told him, "I don't have my own children. I have other goals to work on before I even consider a family."

"What goals, if you don't mind my asking?"

She smiled. "Don't look so skeptical. I'm starting college this fall. A little later than most, but it's something I've always dreamed of."

And could never do, Gavin guessed, hearing her unsaid words, because so much of her money went to Ben to get him out of trouble every time she turned around.

"Between school and working, I won't have time for much of anything else."

"It doesn't sound like it. Does your brother know you've wanted to go to college?"

Her face closed off as if she'd slammed a door. There was that sisterly loyalty again. He had to admire her for it, even if it made him want to shake her.

"I don't know," she said. "It's not something that comes up in everyday conversation."

"It came up in ours," Gavin said. "But knowing Ben, and knowing you, I imagine when the two of you talk, it's about him. What are you going to study?" he asked before she could jump to Ben's defense. She'd been about to; he'd seen it in her eyes.

"I want a degree in accounting."

"That's your thing, isn't it? Numbers?"

"That's my thing."

"You're already a bookkeeper. What will you do once you have your degree?"

She got a faraway look, her eye on a goal only she could see. But she wasn't smiling, didn't look dreamy or eager. Only determined. He could see her coming a mile away.

"I want to be a Certified Financial Planner, someone families can come to for financial advice."

"Because of your parents."

"Ben talks too much."

"Sometimes." Ben had told him how their parents had run their car into a utility pole on their way home from a party, both of them drunk. About the mountain of debts they'd left their two grieving children. How Anna had worked two jobs, sometimes three, to keep the house, feed and clothe her and Ben. How she had fought off the social workers to keep Ben with her.

"It seems to me," Gavin said, "that you could have sold that Harley, and the house, and come out all right. Hell, they weren't your debts anyway. You weren't liable for them."

"Tell that to the bill collectors, the lawyers and the IRS, all of whom came pounding on the door."

"So you want to help other families avoid that."

"That's right."

"You'll be good at it. Because you care."

"Thank you." It was the nicest thing he could have said to her, Anna thought. "I have to admit that ego is part of it."

"Ego? You?"

"I have one, and it's darn tired of having to train college graduates how to be my boss, simply because

I don't have a degree. With a degree and a business of my own I won't have to put up with that nonsense.''

"Smart thinking." He toasted her with his nearly empty glass. "Smart lady."

The waitress spotted his empty glass the instant he put it down and swooped over to cheerfully refill it.

"So what about you?" Anna asked when the waitress finished. She was tired of talking about herself. "Have you ever been married? Do you have any children?"

"No, and no. Someday, maybe, but I'm in no hurry to settle down. I like my life just the way it is." He smiled wryly. "Besides, first I would have to find a woman who's more interested in me than in the number of rock stars I know."

"I don't believe that," Anna scoffed.

"That I know a lot of rock stars?"

"That women only want you for who you know. I can't imagine a woman not being attracted to you."

Gavin grinned at the fierce blush that stained her cheeks as she realized what she'd said. "Yeah?"

Mortified, Anna dabbed at her mouth with her napkin. "Well, uh, I mean, uh, never mind."

"Ah, come on," he teased. "What were you going to say?"

"Absolutely nothing. My lips are sealed."

"I'm crushed." His grin was wide.

"Is this that twelve-year-old-boy ego you spoke of?"

He winced playfully. "Ouch. Okay, truce. Let's just say you like me and I like you." His smile was crooked. "I do, you know. I like you very much, Anna Lee Collins."

He could have no idea, Anna thought, how much

that meant to her. She'd never made friends easily. Friends, and family, too, hurt you. They left you.

Gavin would leave, too, she reminded herself. And soon.

"Now I'm really wounded," he told her. "When a man tells a woman how much he likes her, he doesn't expect her to look so sad."

Anna shook her head and smiled. "Sorry. My mind wandered."

"To someplace sad?"

"It doesn't matter."

"It does to me. I don't want you to be sad. Come on," he said, gesturing with his fork. "Let's think of something fun to do tomorrow."

Anna blinked. "Fun?"

"Yeah, you know, as in having a good time."

"What kind of fun?"

"I don't know. When's the last time you flew a kite?"

Anna chuckled. "Try never."

Gavin's fork clanked against his plate. "You're kidding, right?"

"No. I've never flown a kite."

"Well, now, we'll just have to do something about that."

It was big and bold, five feet wide, seven feet long, divided into three triangles of red, yellow and green, a bright, sassy diamond dancing in the brilliant sky, sporting a ten-foot tail of bright blue bows.

It was Anna's first kite and she was shrieking with delight as the wind tugged hard, threatening to lift her from the ground as she held the spindle tight in both hands.

"Whoa." Gavin laughed with her and put his hands around her waist. "I think I better hold on to you, or that kite's gonna carry you clear across the lake."

The wind, as usual for a warm June day in Oklahoma, was strong out of the south. There were at least a half dozen kites flying from this wide grassy area south of the marina on the east shore of Lake Hefner in far northwest Oklahoma City. Anna appeared to be the only person over the age of ten who was doing it for the first time, but she wasn't worried about it.

She wasn't worried about much of anything just then. Not even the knowledge, via the morning's e-mail, that Ben was definitely in San Francisco could spoil her mood. That just meant Gavin would be with her that much longer.

She knew she was heading for trouble. Her feelings for Gavin were growing by the hour. When he left, as she knew he would, he would leave a hole in her life.

But for now he was beside her and the day was much too glorious for her to be looking for trouble. Out on the lake, windsurfers darted across the wakes of sleek sailboats. On the south shore at Stars and Stripes Park families picnicked, children chased each other and laughed. On the southeast shore, Anna had the wind and sun on her face, the kite soaring high, and Gavin Marshall's hands upon her waist. There had never been a more glorious day.

She hadn't realized how liberating it could be to simply have fun. It was hard to worry about much of anything while flying a kite. Except keeping her kite aloft and out of the water, away from other kites, away from the few trees around that were tall enough to be a threat. Those were the important concerns of the day. Nothing else. Nothing else mattered at all.

"Let it out some more," Gavin urged.

"Are you sure?"

"Come on, live dangerously."

Anna laughed, wondering if he realized she was laughing at herself. Because for her, flying a kite at Lake Hefner on a Sunday afternoon with Gavin Marshall was about as dangerous as Anna's life got.

"Slowly," Gavin cautioned. "Just a little at a time."

"Like this?"

"Just like that. A little more. More. There, that's good."

A clean, tantalizing scent rose from her sun-warmed hair, tempting Gavin to bury his nose against it, press his face into it and just breathe her in. Lord, but the woman was getting to him. Even her sunscreen—SPF gazillion, because Anna didn't take chances—smelled sexy to him.

To take his mind off her, he brought up a subject he'd been curious about since he'd first seen this lake when he'd been out riding around a few days ago. "So tell me what the heck Oklahoma City is doing with all these seagulls?"

"Enjoying them?" Anna offered.

"Uh-huh, but what are they doing here?"

"You don't like seagulls?"

"I like seagulls just fine. But they're usually found near the sea. In case you haven't noticed, Oklahoma is a little on the landlocked side."

Anna laughed and shrugged. "I have no idea how they got here. Maybe they blew up from the Gulf on the remnants of a hurricane."

Gavin pursed his lips. "I hadn't thought of that. That could do it."

"Oh, no! It's dropping," Anna cried, looking up at the kite. "Why is it dropping? I knew we shouldn't have let it out so much."

Gavin laughed. "You did not." He reached for the string a couple of feet above the spindle and gave it jerk. "Come on, try this." He turned her and together they ran while Gavin tugged upward on the string, trying to lift the kite.

The kite drifted upward, but when Anna turned her head to watch, she stumbled, and Gavin tripped over her. They went down together in a tangle of arms, legs and kite string. Gavin managed to roll and avoid landing on top of her, but his arm was still around her waist. She landed on top of him.

Finally, he thought, she was right where he wanted her. In his arms.

The thought startled him. He hadn't known he wanted to hold her, but as he was doing it and it felt so damn good, it was hard to deny.

He had a feeling that if he brought it to her attention that she was nestled snugly between his legs, the startled laughter in her eyes would die, and he didn't want that. Didn't want that at all. So he rolled slightly until she lay beside him on the grass, his arm slipping up behind her neck.

He would have been stunned to know that Anna was disappointed by the move. She was a little stunned herself. Shocked was more like it, to have enjoyed being sprawled on top of him that way. It had been...interesting.

She bit the inside of her lip. Who was she trying to kid? It had just relegated kite flying to the second most dangerous thing she'd ever done. Lying on Gavin's chest, with his hips cradling hers, held the number one spot.

Dangerous. Exciting.

Maybe she was glad after all that that particular contact had been so brief. If she'd had time to think about it she might have had time to get embarrassed.

And maybe he'd shifted her off his chest because he hadn't liked having her there as much as she'd liked being there.

And maybe she was making more out of an innocent accident than she should. It was still a glorious day. She didn't want to ruin it by thinking too much. If she thought, she would start to wonder what it would have felt like if he'd kissed her.

"Ah," he said with a gusty sigh. "This is how kite flying is supposed to be done."

Anna chuckled. "On your back?"

"Exactly. You can watch the kite, look at the clouds and not have to worry about getting a crick in your neck."

Gavin wanted to keep her there next to him, but she wouldn't stay put. He didn't know if he'd made her nervous, or if she was just having too much fun to be still. Whatever the reason, she sprang up and took the spindle with her. Not entirely displeased, Gavin rose slowly and stood beside her.

There would be another time, he vowed, when she would lay in his arms and want to linger.

Down, boy, she's not for you.

That, he admitted, was the absolute, undeniable truth. She was not for him. She wasn't a good-time girl out looking for a little mutual satisfaction. She was the sober and serious Anna Collins who was just now learning how to have fun.

And none of what was running through his mind made him want to hold her any less.

Damn.

They stayed in the park for another hour, until dark clouds started rolling in from the west. Flying a kite over a lake with a thunderstorm on the way being a blatant invitation to a lightning strike, they reeled in the kite and headed for home.

"I guess I can safely assume," Gavin said from the passenger seat of her car, "that you enjoyed kite flying."

The storm was moving in faster now, with purple-gray clouds boiling forward, rapidly eating up the sky.

Anna laughed. "I loved it. It was…exhilarating." At a stoplight on Northwest Sixty-third, she glanced at him and smiled. "Thank you."

Oh, the lady didn't play fair. When a woman said thank you in a voice gone all quiet and husky that way, a man wanted—needed—to kiss her when he said you're welcome.

What the hell, the light was still red. He leaned over and kissed her on the cheek. "You're welcome."

Startled, Anna touched a hand to her cheek, to the very spot where his lips had pressed against her oh, so briefly. Too briefly. She wasn't in the habit of being kissed, on the cheek or otherwise. "What was that for?"

"Just because."

Just because, she thought. *Just because.*

That was probably the reason her heart was suddenly racing. Just because.

By the time they pulled into the driveway, storm

clouds had blocked out the sun. Gavin got out and raised the garage door. Anna barely had the car in the garage before the first sheet of rain swept in.

Tugging the door down and wiping splattered rain from his face, Gavin eyed Anna as she got out of the car. "I repeat—you need an automatic garage door. If that last light had been red, we wouldn't have made it."

She shrugged, closed the car door and headed for the kitchen door. "We could have waited it out. It won't last long. Or we could have gotten wet. I doubt either of us would have melted."

Gavin shook his head and followed her into the house.

True to Anna's prediction, the storm didn't last long. Within an hour it had swept past them, leaving everything shiny clean and wet. "If I were to guess," she muttered, looking out the patio door, "I'd guess the grass loved that rain. I swear it's grown an inch since this morning."

"Maybe I'll take another swipe at it with the mower tomorrow," Gavin told her.

"You don't have to do that," she protested.

"I don't mind. It'll give me something to do. I kind of enjoy feeling useful now and then," he added with a smile.

"You mowed the yard last week," she reminded him. "And fixed my garage door. Just yesterday you washed my car. If you keep on, I'll start to think you're indispensable and won't let you go home at all."

"You'd keep me here?" Tilting his head and studying her, Gavin gnawed on the inside of his jaw. "I think I'll write a song. 'Kidnapped by a Slave-Driving Woman.' It could be a hit."

"And here you've led me to believe you were a *successful* songwriter."

"Why, Anna Lee Collins. You made a joke."

"Why, I guess I did. I don't know what came over me." But she did know. Gavin Marshall had come over her. She just wasn't sure what, if anything, she should—or could—do about it.

The question kept her awake most of the night. She chose to blame her sleeplessness on the second thunderstorm that crashed through at 2:00 a.m.

It really wasn't anything to lose sleep over, this growing feeling inside her for Gavin. It couldn't go anywhere, mean anything. She knew that. It wasn't like her to get all hot and prickly on the inside over a man. Not like her at all.

Still, it was a private thing, something she could, and would, keep to herself. She wouldn't dream of doing anything to let him know how she felt. If she even knew herself what she was really feeling. For surely Gavin Marshall wasn't the least bit attracted to her.

Was he?

No. Other men weren't. It was foolish to think that a walking, talking Adonis of a man like him would be.

No, Gavin was just a very nice man—who happened to cause odd reactions inside her. He'd come into her life to try to help keep her brother out of trouble. He was being nice to her because he was a nice man.

The truth of that tied her stomach in knots and kept her awake until nearly four. When her alarm went off at six-thirty she stumbled from the bed and groped her way toward the bathroom. The light over the mirror blinded her. She squeezed her eyes shut and moved to sit on the toilet lid to gather her wits before turning on the shower. But something went wrong.

The toilet lid wasn't there.

Neither was the seat.

Her shriek of shock as she fell butt-first into the toilet echoed off the tiled walls and spilled out into the rest of the house.

Gavin was certain he'd never moved so fast in his life. One minute he'd been sound asleep; the next, he'd been awakened by a scream. In one leap he was out of bed, through the door and down the hall. He barely had time to register that his heart was thundering in his ears. All he knew was that something terrible had happened.

"Anna? Anna!" He hit the bathroom door in time to see her erupt, fury on her face and in every muscle, from the toilet. From...inside the toilet. Maybe he wasn't as awake as he'd thought, but unless his eyes were deceiving him, it didn't take a rocket scientist to figure out what had happened.

He thought maybe he was in trouble.

She turned toward him. Her fists were clenched at her sides. The back of her nightgown dripped water onto the bath mat. There was murder in her eyes and, when she spoke, a snarl in her voice. "You left the lid up."

"Uh...uh..." What could a man say? The prudent thing to do, he figured, was to retreat. He took a step backward.

"And the seat," she growled, stalking him.

He took another step out into the hall and tried to choke back a snicker. It wasn't funny, he told himself. A woman falling into the toilet really wasn't funny. "Now, Anna."

Anna was so livid she was nearly sputtering with it.

Red spots danced in front of her eyes. The indignity of falling into her own toilet was simply not to be borne. And to have a witness! The guilty party himself! It was just too much. With her fingers curved like claws, she took another step toward him. "Justifiable," she muttered.

"How's that?" His lips were twitching.

"Justifiable homicide. That's what they'll call it."

"Now, Anna." He snickered. "You have to admit—"

"If, that is, they ever find all the pieces of your body."

"I had no idea you were the bloodthirsty type."

She advanced on him again. "Did you know we have a Make My Day law in Oklahoma? Being threatened in my own home gives me the legal right to kill you."

"I'm sorry. I apologize. I'll never leave the seat up again. Come on, Anna, you—"

He couldn't finish, Anna noted, for the simple reason that the sorry creep obviously found the entire incident absolutely hysterical.

"You dare to laugh?" She took another step, desperately afraid she might be starting to see the humor in the situation.

"You have to admit…"

"I don't have to admit anything to a man wearing— Good grief." She squinted to make sure she was seeing correctly. "You sleep in Bugs Bunny boxers?"

"You can't murder a man wearing Bugs Bunny boxers. I'll just, uh, go on back to bed."

With a snarl, she chased him to his bedroom door.

Back in the bathroom she stood in front of the tub and stared down at the water on the mat.

She burst out laughing.

Chapter Nine

"All right, out with it."

In the act of putting her purse away for the day in
the bottom drawer of her desk at work that morning,
Anna paused and looked up.

Donna stood beside the next desk, hands on hips,
eyes narrowed, lips pursed.

Anna slid the drawer shut and straightened. "Out
with what?"

"Last week out of the blue you ask about a rock-
and-roll songwriter, and suddenly you know the names
of songs and artists you never paid any attention to
before. Today you walk in here with a smile on your
sunburned face. You never walk in with a smile, and
you never get sunburned. And you haven't even noticed that we finally got that new filing cabinet we've
been begging for for months."

Amazed that she hadn't noticed, Anna blinked at the

four-drawer lateral file cabinet gracing the wall opposite her desk. "So we did." How could she have
missed it?

"What gives?" Donna demanded. "This is totally
out of character for you."

"It is?" Anna frowned. What did that say about her,
that her co-worker considered a smile from Anna as
out of character? Besides, she wasn't about to admit
that she was smiling about Bugs Bunny boxer shorts
and having fallen into the toilet.

Donna's eyes widened. "Oh, my stars. It's a man."

"Don't be ridiculous. What makes you say a thing
like that?"

"The blush on your cheeks, for one thing."

"Sunburn."

"No dice. You have to tell. Who is he? Where did
you meet him? What's he like?"

"Donna—"

"Anna." Donna tapped her toe against the carpet.
"You are the most levelheaded person I know. Your
moods never change, you're always just straight business. Always. You don't have highs and lows like the
rest of us mortals. Hell's bells, you never even suffer
from PMS. Now you're listening to rock, getting sunburned, smiling, scowling now and evading my questions. It has to be a man."

Anna couldn't help the small smile that bloomed.

"Aha! I knew it."

Grinning, Anna sat at her desk and turned on her
computer. "You don't know anything. There's nothing
to know." The truth of that wiped the smile from her
face. There really was nothing to know. Not the way
Donna meant it.

"Uh-oh," Donna said, noting the change in Anna's expression. "You wanna talk about it?"

Anna's smile came back, bittersweet this time. "There's nothing to tell." *He was on his way out of my life the day he came into it.*

Roast beef. That was the smell that greeted Anna when she stepped into the house that evening. Roast beef in the kitchen, scented candles beside her grandmother's china and silver on the table, and flowers in the living room. A glorious bouquet of carnations, daisies and baby's breath. Any single one of the surprises would have been enough to take her breath. Together, they made her want to cry.

Who was she kidding? The flowers alone had her eyes misting. She'd never received flowers before. Never. Not from anyone. A bittersweet ache bloomed in her chest.

Oh, she could get used to this, to Gavin and his teasing fun, his tender care of her. His sweet, sweet apologies. That's what this was, she knew, an apology for leaving the seat up. Or maybe for laughing at her, she thought, getting her balance back.

"Gavin?"

Her assumption was proved correct a moment later when a white flag—a dish towel—fluttered in the doorway to the hall. "Am I forgiven?"

"I don't know," she said with narrowed eyes when he stepped into the room looking like that twelve-year-old boy they'd talked about. A very sheepish twelve-year-old boy. "Are you going to do it again?"

"No, ma'am." It wasn't hard to tell that he was fighting a smile. "My mother would never forgive me if I got myself murdered for doing something she worked years to break me of."

Still trying to look stern, Anna crossed her arms over her chest. "I'm sure she'd be pleased to hear it." Then she gave up and smiled. "You've been busy. Roast beef?"

"Another one of my mother's lessons."

"And the flowers are beautiful. Thank you."

She was in for more surprises, she soon learned. In her bedroom was another floral surprise, this one a potted fuchsia azalea in full bloom.

"The flowers in the living room are for leaving the seat up," Gavin said from the door.

"And these?"

"For laughing."

The bachelor buttons in the bathroom were for him, he said, to remind him to put the seat down.

Anna was delighted and charmed. He wouldn't even allow her to help clean up after dinner, but escorted her to the living room, where he turned on the History Channel for her to watch. He knew how she liked documentaries.

That the one on the air just then happened to be the history of the Harley-Davidson motorcycle was a mere coincidence. Or so he claimed with a perfectly innocent blink.

When he finished in the kitchen he joined her on the couch. He didn't even swear, although she was sure he wanted to, when he whacked his shin on the coffee table.

She was amazed when he pointed out that the motorcycle featured on the current segment was the same model as Ben's.

"You're kidding. Ben's motorcycle made it into a documentary?"

"His model. Look at it. You can tell it's the same model."

"I hate to sound like a cliché, but they all look pretty much alike to me."

Gavin rolled his eyes. "The Electra Glide that Ben rides is one they upgraded in 1966. Boosted the horsepower. There were less expensive bikes on the market, even from Harley."

Anna gave a crooked smile. "Knowing Daddy, he probably went for the most expensive he could get his hands on, just for the bragging rights."

When the program was over Anna turned to Gavin. "Did you get any news today about Ben?"

Gavin shook his head. "My guess is he's about ready to leave San Francisco by now, if he hasn't already."

"Where would he go from there?"

"Tahoe. Reno. Carson City."

"To gamble."

Gavin let out a long breath. "That's my guess. I'll keep asking around. I remembered a guy I know in Reno and e-mailed him today. If Ben shows up at any of the casinos there, Jerry will let me know."

Discouraged and worried, Anna leaned her head against the back of the couch and closed her eyes.

"Hey, come on," Gavin urged. "He's all right. He'll either turn up here any day, or I'll get word that he's back in L.A. Don't worry about him."

"I can't help it."

Gavin stroked her cheek with the tip of one finger. "I guess you can't. Neither can I, really. But let's think about something else. Worrying won't do either one of us any good."

One corner of Anna's mouth curved up. "Now you tell me. You mean I've had it wrong all these years?"

"Yep. Ice cream, that's the answer."

"I don't have any ice cream."

"Ah, but I do. Or rather, Ben does. Since he's not here, I say we eat it."

Anna opened her eyes. "That sounds like an excellent idea." She pushed herself up from the couch and went to the kitchen.

Gavin rose and followed. "I'm glad you liked that music so much."

She took two cereal bowls out of the cabinet. "What are you talking about?"

"You were humming just now."

"I was? I guess so." She smiled.

"'Angel of Music,' huh?"

"It makes me wish I had Ben's talent for playing by ear." She set the bowls on the counter and placed two spoons beside them. "He could listen to a song one time, then sit down and play it on the piano."

"He's got a gift, I won't deny that. You could learn, take lessons," he suggested.

"They don't give playing-by-ear lessons, as far as I know."

"I meant just learn to play the piano."

Something flickered in Anna's eyes, but she lowered her gaze before Gavin could interpret it.

"Learn to play?" she asked. "Me?"

"Sure. You take some lessons, learn to play, then you could get the sheet music to *Phantom of the Opera* and play it whenever you wanted."

She blinked up at him, took a step toward the den,

toward the piano, as if just the thought of learning to play lured her there. "You think I could?"

"I know you could." He walked with her into the den, to the piano. "Look how smart you are with numbers. You'd pick this up in a snap." Inwardly he winced at what that linear, analytical mind of hers would do with sheet music. He knew she could learn to read and play it, but would any of the composer's emotions come through her add-'em-up-and-total-'em thought processes?

She lifted the top of the piano bench and looked down at the two stacks, one of lesson books, the other of sheet music. "You really think I could learn?"

"I really think you could learn."

The top piece of sheet music was Tchaikovsky's Piano Concerto no. 2. She picked it up. "I could read music and play something like this?"

"Sure," he thought with amused apologies to Tchaikovsky. "You'd have to start with the lesson books, the basics, learn the notes and all. You could work your way up to something like that if you practiced a lot." He didn't want to give her the mistaken impression that it would be easy. But he didn't want to discourage her by telling her that it would be years before she would be able to do justice to the piece in her hands.

She opened the sheet music and stared at it. Over her shoulder he could see it was a difficult arrangement, no simple beginner's version. Assuming Ben had played that piece, and knowing that with Anna hounding him, holding the Harley over his head, he had probably played it damn well, impressed Gavin to no end.

As if in a daze, Anna pulled out the bench. She sat down, placed the music on the piano and opened the keyboard cover. "You really think I could learn to play this?"

Gavin bit back a smile. "Someday." She looked as if she were about to place her hands on the keys and make beautiful music.

"You're sure?"

"Anna, you're not a stupid person. I think you could learn to do anything you set your mind to."

"Even something as complicated as this?"

"How much more complicated can it be than, say, an income statement or a balance sheet? You learned how to do those, you can learn this."

"Well," she said hesitantly, studying the complicated notes on the pages opened in front of her. "If you really think I could, I guess I could give it a try." She placed her hands on the keys.

The opening bars of Tchaikovsky's Piano Concerto no. 2 were powerful. Stirring. And perfectly played.

Anna paused. Peering up over her shoulder at him, she batted her eyes. "Like that?"

"Why, you fraud."

Her grin was evil. "Remember the garden hose? And the toilet seat?" She batted her eyes again and showed her teeth. "Gotcha."

"You low-down, sneaky, lying fraud."

Her eyes widened in outrage. "I never lied. You never asked me if I knew how to play."

"You deliberately let me make a fool out of myself."

Her teeth flashed again in a grin. "Yes. I did."

"Proud of yourself, aren't you?"

"Actually, I am. I've never been very good at practical jokes. Maybe you just bring out the best in me. Don't take it too hard," she added, patting his hand.

"People often assume I'm a no-talent dud because I enjoy something as boring as bookkeeping."

Gavin shook his head and chuckled. "You sure reeled me in."

"Yes, I did."

He shook his head again. "I don't get it. I thought you didn't like music."

"I never said I didn't like it, just that I never had time to listen to it."

"To hear Ben tell it, when your parents were alive the house was always filled with music."

"It was." She looked away.

"But?"

"But nothing. Mama and Daddy listened to music all day and all night. To the exclusion of much else. They used to spend hours, when they were home, just sitting around listening to music."

"While you did what?"

"It's not important, Gavin."

"Tell me. What did you do while they listened to music?"

She gave a little shrug of one shoulder. "Cleaned house, did laundry, cooked."

"How old were you?"

She shrugged again. "About ten when I started taking care of things."

"I guess they more or less left you with a distaste for music. Yet you made Ben stick with it."

"It wasn't that I disliked music. I just resented the time wasted listening to it when so many other things needed to be done. I never had that kind of time to waste. I guess I deliberately blocked music from my life to prove I wasn't like them."

"But you didn't," he protested. "You still play the piano."

"That's different."

"Why?"

"You're a musician. You know how it is."

"Tell me how it is with you."

"It's just…different. Listening to music is passive. Playing it has nothing to do with that. When I play, I'm not wasting time, I'm in control. It's my outlet. When I'm stressed or frustrated or sad or happy…I can express all that through the keyboard. I can't express anything by listening."

"Play the rest of it," Gavin said.

"This?" She waved a hand at the sheet music. "You don't really want to hear this."

"I say I do."

"Fine." With a shrug, she turned back to the keyboard.

She started over from the beginning. She didn't merely strike the correct notes. He knew this piece, had heard it played by pianists, by symphony orchestras. He'd heard it performed by the best. All of that was wiped from his mind as Anna blew him away. His skin prickled, as though lightning were building up to strike.

She played with such power. Such passion. She quite literally held him in awe with her talent and the emotion that came through the keyboard.

She wasn't even reading the music. Her eyes were closed, her head tilted back, neck arched, as she poured herself, her soul, into the music.

Gavin didn't think old Pyotr Tchaikovsky particularly had sex in mind when he penned those particular notes, but sex was what went through Gavin's mind, through his blood, as Anna played. Her passion for the music became his passion for her. His blood sang with it, his loins grew tight and heavy with it. Whether it was the look of intense concentration on her face—a look a woman might have as she rose above a man in the heat of lovemaking—or the sheer passion of the music itself, Gavin's heart pounded with the nearly irresistible urge to take her right then and there. Against the piano, on the bench, on the floor. Anywhere. Everywhere. He didn't care.

Never mind that she wasn't his type, that he had no intention of settling down. This wasn't about settling down, it was about sex, raw and primitive.

The room fairly shook with power, with passion. When the last notes died away, the only sound left was that of Gavin's harsh breathing.

Anna slowly opened her eyes and turned to face him, more than a little wary of his reaction. She knew that she tended to get carried away when she played, especially that particular piece, which was her favorite for the emotional outlet it provided. "What do you think?"

"I think…" His hands cupped her face, sending a shudder down her spine and pulling her from the bench to stand in front of him. "You're magnificent."

Something in his eyes, the heated look in them, and in his voice, the dark rough velvet of it, made her breath catch in her throat.

"And I think that if you don't like what I'm about to do, I'll be ordering up more flowers, but this has been coming on for days, and now it just has to happen." He dipped his head toward her.

Mercy. He was going to kiss her. She'd thought of it, of what it might be like, for days. She'd wanted it, she could admit to herself. But only now, as his strong hands cradled her cheeks and his warm breath brushed her face, did she understand her own need. His touch made the muscles low in her abdomen clench.

Softly, like the wings of a butterfly, his lips brushed hers. Once. Twice. Her heart stopped.

With the tip of his tongue, he stroked her lips. "Open," he whispered. "Open for me, Anna, let me taste you."

Taste. Oh, yes, she wanted to taste him. She parted her lips and welcomed him.

The unpracticed innocence of the way she opened, took him in, shook Gavin. Her taste enticed him. Her heat burned him all the way to his bones. Some part of himself deep inside that he hadn't known was empty began to fill with her, with her warmth, her generosity, her honest, mind-numbing response to his kiss.

Anna.

He took the kiss deeper, devouring her, taking all she gave, giving back all he had to give. He'd had no idea he had so much to give a woman. He forced himself to keep his hands on her face for fear of taking too much of her, but he wanted to touch her, all of her, everywhere. In every way.

Anna.

Her arms slid around his waist, her hands splayed across his back. *Yes! Hold me. Hold on to me.*

She did. She held on for dear life, because if she didn't, Anna knew she would slither to the floor in a puddle of need. She'd been kissed before, but never like this. Never with such tenderness, yet so forcefully. No hands had ever touched her with so much gentleness, yet were so possessive. Her blood had never sang this way, her heart had never soared. He was claiming her, and she was on fire. It both terrified and thrilled

her. Emboldened, and humbled. She could taste his
need of her. Or was that her need of him?

What matter, as long as it never ended. As long as
this exquisite, tormenting pleasure went on forever.

But it didn't, of course. And when he took his lips
from hers it felt as though he were taking some deep,
vital part of her with him.

Gavin felt her shudder. He slid his arms around her
and pulled her close against his chest, reveling in the
feel of her. Never had he felt so much from just a kiss.
Not ever. And it shook him.

She buried her face against his shoulder. He needed
to see her, to look into her eyes, but his need to hold
her tight was stronger. As was his fear. If he looked
into her eyes and didn't see the same wonder he was
feeling, it just might kill him. So he played the coward
and held her close.

"Do I need to call the florist?" he managed, his
breath held in fear of her answer.

With her heart still pounding and her breath still
rasping in her throat, Anna forced herself to lift her
head and look at him. She wasn't a particularly brave
woman, but never had so much been at stake. Her voice
came out in a whisper. "If you mean to apologize, I'll
be insulted."

His smile came slowly, curving his mouth first, then
lighting his eyes to brilliant blue. Stealing her breath.
"Yeah?"

With a sigh, she smiled and laid her head back on
his shoulder, tilted it to look up at him. "Yeah."

"Good." The temptation was too great. Her lips
were too near. The invitation in her eyes irresistible.
He kissed her again, taking her mouth with his, invading her, mating his tongue with hers. She made a low

sound of pleasure in her throat that went straight to his head.

God, she felt so good pressed against him. So good, so right. He didn't question the sense of it, because sense didn't matter. Only kissing her mattered, tasting her, holding her. Touching her.

Anna reveled in his touch. When his hands slid down her back to cup her hips she nearly groaned in pleasure at the heated sensations engulfing her. Her mind went numb, and she didn't care. Refused to care. Nothing mattered but this. This intense pleasure.

She wasn't sure how her shirttail came to be free, but the feel of his hot, hard hands on her flesh left no room to worry about it. Everywhere he touched, she tingled. His hands devoured her, as did his mouth. And then one of those hands cupped her breast and the feeling was so exquisite that her knees turned to jelly. She threaded her fingers through his hair and held on, with no will to do anything other than go on kissing him, be kissed by him, forever.

Gavin treasured the weight of her breast. He barely stopped short of pushing her bra aside to feel that soft, warm flesh against his palm.

Realizing how close he was to losing control, he forced his hand to release her and slip from beneath her blouse. Forced himself to release her lips, those soft, generous lips that tasted sweeter than any wine.

They stood together, held each other, until hearts calmed, pulses leveled. Then, as if by mutual agreement, they stepped apart.

Gavin wanted, very much, to kiss her again. Her lips were still red and puffy from the pressure of his. Her eyes, as wide and gray as a misty mountain lake, mesmerized him, drew him. So trusting, those eyes, but he didn't feel at all trustworthy just then. "I think," he said slowly, regretfully, his hands trailing up and down her arms, "I'm going to turn in now before I get us both in trouble here."

She wanted to protest. She wanted to ask him to kiss her again. Better yet, she yearned for the courage to stretch up and kiss him herself. But she'd never had a lot of courage, and what little she'd had a few minutes ago seeped away. Unable to hold his gaze, she stepped back and looked away. "All right," she told him softly. "Good night, then."

His hands trailed down her arms one last time, his fingers lingering on hers as though he didn't want to let go. A sweet, sweet ache bloomed in her chest. And as he turned to go, she knew that her earlier determination to keep her growing feelings for him to herself had been a wise one. Now there was real cause for terror. She'd done the unthinkable. She'd fallen in love with him.

Who would have thought that kissing Anna Lee Collins would be such a powerful experience?

Gavin stared toward the ceiling in the darkness of his room and laughed silently at himself. He must have thought it would be great or he wouldn't have been so intrigued by her all these days.

No, that wasn't right. It was her, all of her, the woman, who had intrigued him, not just the thought of kissing her. So rigid and uptight, so straitlaced and unbending. So loyal toward that idiot brother of hers. Yes, she had intrigued him from the beginning. From before he'd ever met her, before he'd barged his way into her home. He'd been fascinated by the stories Ben had told of how she had managed to pull the two of them out of the hole their parents had left them in, how she had challenged him to finish school, forced him to learn to play the piano.

Gavin knew Ben Collins. Getting the kid to do anything that was good for him was damn near impossible. Gavin had known from the beginning that Anna Collins must be some kind of miracle worker. She'd sure worked a miracle or two on him since he'd hit Oklahoma. He'd been there, what, a week and a half? And just now realized he hadn't been to a single party. Hadn't missed going. At home he would have been to half a dozen in that amount of time.

He hadn't had a single beer, and hadn't missed it, either. He'd have gone through a case by now at home.

He hadn't made love to a woman. But hell, it'd been a damn sight longer than a week and a half since he'd done that, and now, tonight, he *really* missed it. But not just sex. Sex was fine. Sex was wonderful. But it was Anna he wanted, and he wanted more than sex. With her he wanted to make love.

The very idea of everything he wanted from Anna scared him. He wasn't ready for all these deep feelings trying to take hold. Didn't want them. Wouldn't allow them, by damn. If he and Anna happened to share a night or two together before he left, well, that would be great. He didn't want more than that. Didn't need more.

Or so he told himself.

Anna thought she could handle it, this being in love. She thought she could cope. But by the time she got to work the next morning she was more miserable than she'd ever been in her life.

Donna, who had pretty much left Anna to her own

devices during the three years they'd worked together, must have decided that Anna had been left on her own long enough. The payroll clerk took one look at her Tuesday morning and let out a disgusted snort.

"Tell me it's not a man, will you."

Anna decided her misery over Gavin must show on her face.

"If there's one thing I know about other than my job, it's men," Donna said stoutly. "Whatever he did to you, throw the bum out. He's not worth it."

Anna had never had a confidante, someone to tell her troubles to. She didn't know that she was ready to have one now. Better to keep her troubles to herself and avoid the embarrassment of looking like a fool. She sat at her desk and put her purse away in the back of the bottom drawer. "I don't know what you're talking about."

"I'm talking about your pale cheeks, red-rimmed eyes with dark circles underneath, and the way you've got your blouse buttoned wrong."

Baffled, Anna looked down at her blouse, turned away from Donna and redid the buttons just above her waist.

"I know you," Donna said firmly. "You would never come to work with a less than perfect appearance. You never have, until now. You know if you don't talk about it you're going to burst. If you don't want to talk to me, okay. We've never been bosom buddies. I can live with that." Her voice softened. "But, Anna, you need to talk to somebody. You're hurting."

Yes. Oh, yes, Anna thought. She was hurting. But it wasn't Gavin's fault.

Suddenly she needed to talk. Desperately. She got up and closed the door to their office.

Donna slowly uncrossed her arms. "Anna?"

Anna returned to her seat and took a moment to gather her nerve. "I...I have this friend," she began, chickening out at the last minute.

"A friend?"

"That's right." Anna moistened her lips. "A friend. She's met someone."

"A man."

"Yes, a man. He's...he's very special." Anna caught herself starting to smile. "But he's temporary. Only in town long enough to conduct a little business, then he'll go home to California."

"Uh-huh. And this, uh, friend of yours," Donna said in a tone that said she saw right through the pathetic ploy but was willing to play along. "She's maybe getting a little too attached, shall we say?"

Anna did smile this time, poignantly, as she gazed off into middle space. "She's in love with him."

"Damn."

"For the first time in her life, she's totally, completely in love. And he'll be gone soon, probably in a couple of days."

Donna was quiet for a moment. Through the paper-thin walls the sound of the copy machine firing up sounded loud.

"How does he feel about...her?" Donna asked.

Anna blinked, sighed. "He likes her well enough, I suppose."

"But he's not in love with her?"

"Of course not. Why would he be?"

Donna shrugged. "Why wouldn't he be? Has she told him how she feels? Asked him how he feels?"

"To what point? He's leaving."

"Does he talk about leaving?"

Anna frowned. "No, but..."

"Forget the but. He doesn't talk about leaving. Maybe he won't."

"He will. He has a life to go back to, a successful career. And I—my friend, well, she's nothing special."

"That's crap."

Startled, Anna blinked. "I beg your pardon?"

"If that's what she thinks of herself, that she's nothing special, she might as well hang it up and send him on his way. If she hasn't got any more faith in herself than that, it's for sure he probably doesn't love her."

Anna's stomach tied itself in a knot. "She's never had much self-confidence."

"What are you doing with a friend like that?" Donna cried, throwing a hand in the air in disgust. "She sure doesn't sound anything like you."

"What do you mean? I..."

"I mean, Anna, dear, that you always know exactly what you want and you've never let anything stand in the way of getting it. You're so damn confident on the job, it's intimidating to the rest of us mortals."

Anna was shaking her head before Donna finished. "You've got it all wrong."

"I don't. And I'll tell you something else. If you're—I mean, if your friend is really in love with this guy, then it's already too late to avoid a kick in the teeth, if that's what's going to happen. If it was me, or you, I'd say you ought to enjoy the ride while you can."

"No." Anna shook her head. "When he leaves, I—she'll be devastated."

"So what? Looks to me like she's already devastated. Better to have loved and lost, and all that."

"That," Anna told her steadily, "is a cliché."

"Clichés get to be clichés because over and over again, people find that they're true. Your friend should hold on to this guy for all she's worth, if she really loves him. Who knows? Maybe she'll find out that he's just as crazy about her."

"What good would that do?" Anna asked quietly. "He still has to go home."

"I'm thinking of another cliché here. True love always finds a way?"

Anna chuckled sadly and shook her head. "I don't think so, but thanks for the advice. And the ear."

"You're welcome. And tell your friend that she's out of her mind if she gives up on love one minute sooner than she has to. She should enjoy him while she has him. And I mean that in every way possible, if you get my drift."

It sounded lovely to Anna, lovely and sad. But she knew she didn't have the courage it would take to bury her fear and simply enjoy being with Gavin. Surely he would see right through her and know how she felt about him. Then he would feel sorry for her, and that she could not bear.

No, she thought. Better to distance herself now. There was no point in anything other than polite friendliness between them. No point at all. Ben would be home soon.

Chapter Ten

By the time Anna pulled into her driveway that evening her nerves were stretched taut and her stomach was churning. She'd worried all day about how to act around Gavin, what, if anything to say to him. How did a woman behave around a man when she didn't want him to know she'd done the unthinkable and fallen in love with him?

She couldn't let him find out. A man like him, the kind of life he surely led in California... The rock-and-roll songwriter and the mousy bookkeeper from Oklahoma. It was laughable. Pathetic. He would, at best, feel sorry for her. At worst, he would laugh at her. Maybe secretly, behind her back.

No, that wasn't right. It didn't fit the Gavin she knew. The man she knew wouldn't deliberately hurt her, wouldn't be cruel.

Neither, she believed with all her aching heart,

would he be willing, or able, to return her feelings. He had an entire other life in California, one he would be returning to soon.

Oh, damn, why did she have to go and mess everything up by falling in love? They'd been having such fun. He'd opened her mind and her eyes to so many things she'd been missing in her life. Things like laughter, *Phantom of the Opera*, kites.

And that, she thought, was one reason she'd fallen for him. He'd taught her how to have fun. Taught her that having fun was important.

She wondered if she would even know how to have fun, much less be capable of it, after he left.

A car pulled up across the street at the Robertses' and revved its engine, making her aware that she'd been sitting in her driveway for several minutes staring at her garage door.

She should never, ever, have gotten close to Gavin Marshall.

She got out of her car and raised the garage door. Gavin stood on the other side, as though reaching to raise the door himself.

"There you are," he said. "You sat out here so long I…" Deep furrows appeared on his brow. Placing his hands gently on her arms, he studied her face. She could swear she felt his gaze like a warm, caring caress. "What's wrong?" he asked.

"Nothing." She tried for a smile, but failed miserably. "I…"

"Anna." He jiggled her arms slightly. "Something's wrong. What is it? Is it Ben? Did he call you at work? Did he show up?"

"No," she said quickly. "No. I haven't heard from him."

Gavin read the truth of that in her eyes. She would always protect her brother the best she could, but she was a lousy liar. She hadn't heard from Ben. But something was wrong. The anguish in her eyes, which she was trying unsuccessfully to hide, hurt him. "Then what is it?" he asked again.

She glanced away. "Nothing." Slipping from his loose grasp, she turned away. "I better get the car put up and dinner started. I don't know about you, but I'm hungry."

He had thought he was, but at her blatant evasion, he found himself rapidly losing his appetite. Except for her. His hunger for her had been gnawing at him all day. All week, if he was being honest. Right now the hunger raged not so much in his loins as in his heart.

This time when the alarm bells went off in his head at the thought of how much Anna was coming to mean to him, he ignored them. He was tired of worrying about what he should want, tired of denying what he did want.

She was hurting, and he was very much afraid it was because of him.

With a sick feeling in the pit of her stomach, Anna changed clothes, then left her bedroom and went to the kitchen. She wasn't the least hungry, but she would eat because Gavin would notice if she didn't and might ask why. She needed to keep everything normal. Normal and calm. It was the only way she was going to survive the rest of Gavin's stay without breaking in two.

She was at the sink scrubbing two baking potatoes for the microwave when Gavin joined her. "I thought

I'd keep it simple tonight," she offered politely. "Salmon patties, baked potatoes and tossed salad."

"Anna—"

"Oh, and corn-on-the-cob. How does that sound?"

"Talk to me," he said.

"All right." She turned off the water and took a fork from the cutlery drawer, then started poking holes in the potatoes. "What would you like to talk about?"

"About why," he said quietly yet firmly, "you're suddenly treating me like a stranger."

"I don't know what you mean."

Gavin reached across her and covered her hands with his, stilling them, feeling, she was sure, the way they trembled. "Last night you said an apology would insult you. What do I do, then, Anna? How do we get back to where we were yesterday before I kissed you?"

Anna stared at his large, dark hands covering her much smaller, paler ones on the sink divider. "Is that what you want?" she asked, her throat aching. "To go back to before you kissed me? To pretend it never happened?"

"If that's what will make you smile at me again."

She swallowed hard. If he moved his fingers less than an inch he would feel how her pulse raced. "Smile?"

"Look at me," he said softly.

She didn't want to. She'd been avoiding looking him in the eye for fear he would be able to read exactly how she felt about him. But at his soft plea she could do nothing but comply.

"What happened, Anna?" With his free hand he touched her cheek. "What's wrong? What did I do to make you push me away?"

"Nothing." She shook her head. "You didn't do anything. I'm not pushing you away."

"It sure feels like it to me."

She couldn't take his nearness anymore without doing something completely foolish, such as laying her head on his shoulder and weeping for all they could not have.

"I'm sorry." She turned away and placed the potatoes in the microwave. "I guess I've just had a lot on my mind today, worrying about Ben, about when he's going to get here."

"Are you in a hurry for him to get here? For me to leave? Is that it?"

"No," she protested quickly. Too quickly, she feared. "I mean, no, I'm not in a hurry for you to leave. But we both know you can't stay here forever. How much longer will you give him? What if he doesn't come at all? If he finds out you're here he's likely to stay away on purpose just to avoid you." She took a deep breath around the knot in her throat. "Maybe I should—"

"No."

At the harsh word, she turned toward him. "You don't even know what I was going to say."

"Don't I?" The muscle along his jaw flexed. "You were going to offer to pay me the cash he owes me. I told you before, it's not your debt. I won't take your money. I thought we were past that, dammit."

"How can we be," she asked quietly, trying to keep the emotions from invading her voice, "when that's the only reason you're here?"

His eyes, those wild blue eyes, pierced her. "Is it?"

"What's that supposed to mean?" she demanded. "You know it is."

"Look." He sighed and ran his splayed fingers through his hair. "Yes, I came here looking for Ben. But dammit, Anna, something else is going on here between you and me. Or it was until I blew it. I'm sorry for that. More sorry than you'll ever know."

"You're sorry you kissed me?"

"Not for a minute." He stuffed his hands into his pockets. "But it seems you are. That's what I'm sorry about."

It would be best for both of them if she let him think she was sorry he'd kissed her, but Anna didn't have it in her to let the lie live. "I'm not sorry, Gavin."

Slowly Gavin pulled his hands from his pockets. "You're not?"

Gathering every ounce of courage she could find, Anna shook her head.

Easy, Gavin cautioned himself. He had to go easy. When what he wanted to do was grab her up in his arms and kiss her again. "Then what's wrong?" He couldn't keep himself from slipping his arms around her.

When he moved to pull her close, she wrenched away. "Don't," came from her lips in a panicked whisper.

She might as well have slapped him. Pride demanded that he turn and walk away. If she didn't want his touch, fine. He wouldn't bother her with it again.

But other emotions, the ones that had weakened his knees the night before when he'd kissed her, held him firm. Demanded that he not give up so easily what they'd shared. "Don't what?" He tried to keep the nerves from his voice. "Don't touch you?"

She closed her eyes and took a long, slow breath. When she opened them again, she refused to meet his gaze. "Under the circumstances, I think that would be best."

Sometime during the last few seconds it had become vital for Gavin that he not let her push him away so easily. Not let her push him away at all. Didn't she know? Didn't she have any idea how rare it was for two people to experience what they'd experienced last night when they'd kissed? How could she turn away from that?

"To hell with circumstances." Fear came out in his voice as anger. "Best for who?"

"For both of us."

Her face paled. He was sorry for that, but he wasn't going to back off. "That's bull and you know it," he told her. "This is what's best." He snared her arm and pulled her to his chest. Her eyes flew wide. She opened her mouth. He swallowed whatever protest she might have voiced by the simple, gratifying method of covering her mouth with his.

The whimper that came from her throat might have caused him a moment's hesitation except that he recognized that it was not a sound of protest. It was an expression of need, of want, of surrender. He tasted it on her lips and tongue, felt it in the way she melted against him almost instantly. Felt it, all of it, inside himself. This was right. This was the way they belonged—together, body to body, mouth to mouth, heart to heart.

The realization shook him. But not enough for him to let go of her.

The kiss and all it meant, all that it made her want, shook Anna. More than enough to have her tear her mouth free and gasp for air, for sanity.

Gavin wasn't having it. As if her mouth were a magnet, his lips followed, reaching again for hers.

"No," she cried, pushing on his chest with both hands. "Don't do this."

He released her so quickly that she stumbled backward against the kitchen counter.

"Don't what?" he demanded. "Don't kiss you? Don't want you? The kissing I can control if I have to. The wanting I can't. It's not something I can just turn on and off. I don't want to turn it off. I don't want to stop wanting you. Don't tell me you don't feel the same, because we both know you'd be lying, and you're a lousy liar, Anna."

"It doesn't matter what either one of us feels," she cried.

"The hell it doesn't. It's the only thing that matters."

"Don't swear at me, Gavin Marshall, just don't you swear at me."

"Then don't try to convince me you weren't kissing me back just then, and loving it every bit as much as I was."

"It doesn't matter," she repeated, her heart breaking. "Gavin, you're leaving. Any day you'll pack up that ratty duffel bag of yours and take yourself out of here. None of this will matter then. You'll leave me the way everyone leaves me. My parents, my brother. Every time I let someone get close to me they leave. I can't even keep the same plumber for longer than a year," she cried. "So what's the point?"

Her words shouldn't have surprised him. Didn't, really. She was right, he would leave. But the emotion in her voice, the pain he heard, twisted in his chest like a knife sunk in to the hilt. "Yes, I'll have to leave soon. I have a career, responsibilities to other people, to myself. Is that supposed to mean that we just— what? Turn our backs on whatever this is that's happening between us and pretend it doesn't exist? Not even give it a chance, give us a chance to enjoy each other while we can?''

"A chance," she said woodenly, turning away from him at the ding of the microwave.

"Is that what you want?" He grabbed her by the arm and pulled her around until she faced him. "Promises? Some sort of guarantee that everything will work out? You want me to tell you I love you?"

"Not unless you mean it."

"I won't say it—wouldn't—unless I mean it. I can't say it to you because I just don't know," he said earnestly. "I've never been in love before. Maybe that's what all this is leading to, but how can we tell if we don't give it a chance? Give *us* a chance? For crying out loud, Anna, we've known each other barely two weeks."

Two weeks? It seemed, to Anna, like a lifetime, as though he'd always been there. Except that she could recall all too clearly how empty her world had been before he'd barged in with his wild blue eyes and his smile that took her breath away. She swallowed hard around the lump in her throat. Two weeks. She'd only known him two weeks. "You make me feel foolish."

"I never meant—"

"No, you're right. We barely know each other." So maybe, she thought with a debilitating combination of hope and dread, maybe she wasn't really in love with him at all. Maybe she was merely infatuated.

Thoughtful now, she turned back to the microwave and removed the potatoes. After wrapping them in foil and setting them aside, she squared her shoulders and faced Gavin.

"I'm sorry. I've been overreacting, acting like a fool."

"Ah, come on, now…" He reached for her.

Anna braced her hands against his chest. "That doesn't mean I'm ready to take up where we left off last night."

Gavin sighed and rested his forehead against hers. "Maybe you're right. Maybe I'm trying to rush things." He raised his head and gave her a crooked smile. "What do you say we just take it slow and see what our guts tell us?" His smile widened. "My gut's telling me we could make beautiful music together."

Anna groaned at the atrocious pun, then let out a chuckle as she stepped back. "That's terrible. I think your gut's telling you it hasn't been fed lately. That," she said, returning his smile, "I'm willing to do something about."

As she turned away to start dinner, Gavin felt a wave of panic threaten to swamp him. He'd just agreed—suggested, damn his hide—that they would slow things down between them. But she was right, he would have to leave soon. How were they supposed to know if this thing between them was as powerful as he thought it was if they didn't give it a chance? And they were running out of time.

But then, maybe he was in this alone. Maybe she didn't feel what he felt, that sharp kick in the gut when he looked into her eyes or heard her laugh, or watched her frown.

He couldn't leave her without knowing if what he felt was real. If she felt it, too. This was too important. *Sorry, Anna, but it looks like I lied to both of us. I'm not going to pull back. I'm going to come after you with everything I've got. Because I have to know. I have to know if this is real.*

"You want to go where?"

Gavin had expected the shock, the resistance. It had taken him all day after their talk last night to come up with the perfect way to keep Anna off balance. If it was calculating of him, so be it. He wanted her off balance. Wanted her so off balance that she fell directly into his arms. Only then would he know the truth.

And if tonight didn't throw her off enough to have her lowering her guard and letting him in, then he would at least be assured that he'd shown her a good time.

"Frontier City," he said with a smile. "It's an amusement park up north of town."

Anna gave him a look of exasperation. "I know what and where it is. I'm just surprised, that's all."

Stunned was more like it, if he read her expression correctly. Stunned, and wary. Leery, even. "How many times have you been there?" he asked.

"Been? To Frontier City? Me?"

"No, I'm talking to the dog across the street. Yes, you."

"There's no need for sarcasm."

God, he loved it when she got all prim and prissy.

"I've never been," she stated rather proudly.

"That's what I figured," he said with a laugh.

"And why," she asked, "did you figure it?"

"Because you never do anything just for fun. That's what tonight is for. Just for fun."

She smiled then, slowly, her eyes lighting. "Will I have as much fun as flying a kite?"

"Guaranteed."

"Then just let me change clothes, and I'll be ready to go."

"Wear jeans," he called as she headed for the bedroom.

She put on jeans, sneakers and a short-sleeved summer sweater tucked in at the waist. She was ready to go in ten minutes.

What she was not ready for, when they reached the garage, was the mode of transportation he'd selected.

"You won't need your purse," he told her.

She narrowed her eyes in suspicion. "Why not?"

"Number one, you don't want to be lugging it around all evening. Number two, we're taking the Harley."

"Not on your life."

Gavin tilted his head and studied her. "You've never ridden it." No need to ask. The truth was in her eyes.

"With good reason," she stated flatly.

"Name one."

"It's too dangerous."

"Says who?"

"Everybody," she said, waving an arm.

"Name one authority that states, and backs up with facts, that riding a motorcycle is more dangerous than any other mode of transportation."

"I don't have to name one. I can see for myself."

Gavin shook his head. "Of all the things you've faced in your life, I can't believe you're going to let something so ordinary as a motorcycle get the best of you."

She crossed her arms over her chest. "It's not getting the best of me. And neither are you. We can take my car."

"Chicken?"

"Sensible."

"Chicken. Come on," he urged. "You're the one who reminded us both that I'll be leaving soon. And I will. I got an e-mail from Jerry this afternoon. Ben's in Reno."

Anna grappled with mixed feelings. She wanted Ben to get away from the gambling. She wanted to see him, talk to him. But she wasn't ready for Gavin to leave yet. "Is he coming home?"

"That's my guess. He knows I'm looking for him now, but he doesn't know I'm here."

"Maybe he'll go back to L.A."

Gavin shook his head, his eyes somber. "He was losing all night last night at the craps tables. He's going to come here for money. Don't let him ruin this one night for us. He'll get here when he gets here. Ride with me, Anna."

Anna shivered. The way he said it—*Ride with me*—his voice soft and husky, brought visions of pale bodies gleaming on dark sheets. Shocked at the images in her brain, she started to flatly refuse. Then she shocked herself again by saying, "All right. But if you kill me on this thing, I promise I'll come back to haunt you."

"Atta girl. I'll even let you wear the helmet."

"Of course you will, since I'm sure the only reason you brought one is because they're required in some states."

"You got that right."

Anna looked up at him, concern replacing humor in her eyes. "It doesn't seem wise to take such a risk with your life as to ride a motorcycle without a helmet."

Gavin stroked her cheek with a thumb. "I suppose not, to someone who thinks she doesn't believe in risks.

I'm flattered that you'd worry for me. But I weigh the risk, and I chose, when I can, to have the wind in my hair. Helmets are too damn hot and heavy, as you're about to find out.''

At the reminder that she had actually agreed to ride that beast of a motorcycle, Anna's mouth dried out. As Gavin slipped the helmet onto her head and fastened the chin strap, her hands started to shake. "I'm, uh, not too sure about this.''

Since he happened to have both hands beneath her chin just then, he used them to tilt her head up until she met his gaze. She expected to see laughter in his eyes, but it wasn't there. Only a tenderness that made her heart ache.

"Trust me, Anna,'' he said quietly. "I would never, ever, do anything to hurt you.''

He wouldn't have kissed her on the lips, or so he told himself, but the helmet was so big on her that it nearly covered her cheeks.

Before he kissed her the way he wanted to—and ran the risk of really scaring her—he turned and mounted the Harley. With a hand held out to her, he said, "Come on. Swing your leg over and let's go have some fun.''

The seat was higher and wider than it looked. By the time Anna was mounted behind Gavin she was out of breath.

"Put your feet here, and here,'' he instructed. "Now comes the fun part—snuggle right up against my back and wrap your arms around me.''

"I bet you say that to all the girls.''

"Why, Anna Collins.'' He grinned at her over his shoulder. "You made another joke.''

She pursed her lips. "Did I?''

Gavin laughed. "I don't have a bike of my own these days. It's been a long time since I've had anyone on behind me. You really do need to hang on," he added.

She knew that. She was afraid enough of riding on the back of this testosterone-pumped bicycle that she had every intention of holding on tight. She just wished that it didn't feel so wonderful to slip her arms around him and press herself against his broad back.

When he started the engine it rumbled to life with that throaty growl peculiar to the Harley-Davidson motorcycle. As Ben had explained to her time and again, there was no other sound quite like it.

There was also, to Anna's way of thinking, nothing quite like feeling all that power come to life beneath her. The vibration shot through to her core, at once terrifying her and thrilling her.

Then the motorcycle moved, and she squeezed her eyes shut and wrapped her arms around Gavin as tightly as she could.

She was sure she was going to die.

Her heart had trouble keeping a steady rhythm for the first couple of miles. Long before they hit the interstate, however, she realized she was not going to die. There was something hedonistic about sitting astride that much power. Like riding the back of a sleek jungle cat, its wildness held in check by the barest of threads and the will of the man in front of her.

Yes. Heady. Wild. Erotic.

And Gavin was right. The helmet was uncomfortably hot and incredibly heavy. Sweat stung her scalp, and her neck was starting to ache. But Anna knew she didn't have the nerve to take it off to relieve the ache and let the wind have her hair.

It was barely six-thirty when they reached the parking lot of Frontier City. The sun was still high and hot. When Gavin killed the engine and Anna climbed off the back of the beast, her legs wobbled.

"Easy does it," he said, but he saw the excitement in her eyes and knew she'd loved the ride. Maybe almost as much as he'd enjoyed feeling her wrapped around his back like skin over muscle. *Thank you Mr. Harley and Mr. Davidson.*

It was a night of magic. The park was crowded with families, teenagers on the loose, couples on dates. People everywhere, of every possible description, laughing, eating, riding the rides, having fun. Gavin pulled Anna right into the thick of it.

At an especially shrill shriek, they looked across a small pond to see a teenage girl falling from a tall tower, nothing between her and certain death but a bungee cord.

"The Geronimo Skycoaster."

"I'm not doing that." Anna took a step back from the wooden railing surrounding the pond. "I'm not doing that."

Gavin slung his arm around her shoulders and laughed. "Me neither. People say I'm crazy, but nobody's ever called me insane. Ah, but look at that," he said, pointing. "Did you say you were hot?"

Anna followed the direction of his pointing finger to see what looked like a hollowed-out log filled with people come speeding down a rail into the pond, water flying everywhere, raining down on the riders. "Uh, Gavin..."

"Come on. I do believe the Log Flume is calling our name."

And so it began. As Anna stepped into the "log" and Gavin slipped in behind her, she kept reminding herself of Donna's words. *Enjoy the ride while you can.* Tonight Anna intended to take that advice literally. Even if it killed her.

It didn't kill her. It was fun.

The ride took them around the carousel, through an admittedly fake-looking wilderness area, and through a covered bridge. Anna was just starting to relax when, in front of her, the ground dropped away. She'd all but forgotten the plunge into the water at the end of the ride. She screamed all the way down, with Gavin's laughter in her ears. She screamed again when they hit the water and it spewed up and rained down on them. When the car pulled to a slow stop at the end of the ride a moment later, her knees were so weak that Gavin had to help her out.

She was grinning like an idiot. "Can we go again?"

Gavin hugged her to his side and laughed. "We can go as many times as you want. What say we try a few other rides while we dry off, then come back."

Ridiculously disappointed at not getting to experience that heart-stopping plunge again, Anna nonetheless agreed.

Her disappointment was swiftly forgotten at the next ride. They hit the Prairie Schooner, and snickered over the play on words. It wasn't a covered wagon, but a stomach-jarring, up-and-down, backward-and-forward ride on a pirate ship.

The Time Warp left her breathless as they swung up and over, dangling for an endless moment upside down high above the park. Anna squeezed Gavin's hand with bruising strength and screamed. She loved it.

They hit them all, the Swingin' Six Guns that flew

them out and around with centrifugal force on the end of what looked like a pitifully weak steel arm. The Silver Bullet with its huge, death-defying loop more than sixty feet in the air and Lord only knew how fast. The Terrible Twister, the Wildcat. And more water at the Renegade Rapids—a giant inner-tube ride down man-made rapids.

They watched the staged gunfight at the OK Corral and ate cotton candy. At the Ring Toss, Gavin won Anna a small stuffed monkey.

They hit the milder rides, the Tilt-A-Whirl, even the carousel. The evil gleam in Gavin's eyes as he rammed into her in the Dodge City Bumper Cars had Anna screaming with delight as she spun her wheel and gave as good as she got.

Then it was back to heart-pounding thrills on the Wardance, the Sidewinder, the Diamond Back—all the scary, thrilling stuff in one ride as it took them backward and forward, tossing them into a three-sixty loop in the middle of both trips and plastering them into their seats with the sheer force of gravity.

"Food," Anna begged as she wobbled away from the Diamond Back and past the Old West buildings fashioned after a frontier town. "I can't keep this up without food."

Grinning, Gavin placed a knuckle beneath her chin and studied her face. "After that ride, your stomach can handle food?"

"I'm starving."

He startled her with a quick kiss on the lips. "I love a woman with a strong stomach."

"Yeah, well, this stomach just got word from my nose that there's barbeque around here somewhere."

Following their noses they found the Santa Fe BBQ

Restaurant in the geographically impossible location right next to the OK Corral, which everyone knew, Anna informed him, was nowhere near Santa Fe.

Gavin tweaked her nose. "We're going to the Old Time photo place and you can be the schoolmarm."

"Pardon me, little lady." A tall, lanky young man in a white cowboy hat, wearing a six-shooter strapped to his thigh and a tin star on his chest, stepped out in their path. "Is this here varmint a'botherin' you?"

Snickering, Anna recognized him as one of the stunt-men/actors from the earlier gunfight. "Gee, I don't know," she told him, batting her eyes. "Is he wanted for anything?"

Playing along, the "sheriff" stroked his chin with thumb and forefinger, studying Gavin through narrowed eyes. "Face looks kinda familiar. Mighta seen him on a Wanted poster."

"Not me, Sheriff, honest." Delighted with Anna's response to the fun, Gavin held up both hands. "It was my evil twin brother who robbed that stage. I'm an innocent man."

"Humph. Just see that you stay that way, young fella."

When he moseyed off to hassle a man drinking a beer, Anna collapsed against Gavin in laughter.

By the time they finished eating, the sun was going down, firing the western sky in a dozen different shades of red, coral, mauve and rose.

"Perfect." Gavin grasped her hand and took her to the Ferris wheel. He was disappointed to realize the cars on this one were built to accommodate several people seated in a circle facing each other. He didn't want to share the ride with strangers. There were certain aspects of a Ferris wheel ride that were, in his book, not to be tampered with.

He got lucky when they ended up the first in line for the next car. He nudged Anna on board, stepped on behind her, then turned back to the attendant and blocked the gate. "Come on, man, have a heart."

The attendant, a forty-something man with a balding forehead and biceps the size of tree trunks, peered over at Anna, then shook his head. "I got rules."

Disappointed, but not defeated, Gavin let the man seat them and lower the bar to hold them in. Then the man turned back and stepped out of the car. "Course, I don't gotta follow 'em." With a wink, he closed the gate and sent them off on their own.

"Nice man." Gavin settled back and slipped his arm around Anna's shoulders, pulling her close to his side as they advanced to let the next in line board the following car.

Anna grinned up at him. "Do you always get what you want?"

"I try my best."

As they slowly rose, notch by notch as the other cars filled, they looked out over the crowds, the rides, the games. The glorious sunset.

Anna thrilled to it all, knowing she would remember this night for the rest of her life. "Thank you for tonight," she said to him.

With the cars filled, the wheel started its lazy turn, taking them slowly up toward the top to the accompaniment of tinny calliope music.

Gavin leaned his head down toward hers. "I'm glad you're having fun." He meant to kiss her lips, but she turned her head at the last instant. "Anna?"

Anna looked up at him and it seemed they were the

only two people in the world as the ground fell away
below, with nothing but a darkening sky above and the
warm southern breeze in their faces.

"Kiss me, Anna."

Once again Donna's words echoed in her mind. *Enjoy the ride while you can.* Arching her neck to reach
him, she whispered, "Yes."

As the Ferris wheel crested and started a slow de-
scent, their lips met. The fire that shot to the pit of her
stomach reminded Anna of the night she had handed
him the phone and their hands had brushed. Sparks.
Electricity.

They'd been heading toward this night even then.
Toward this magical time out of time, when nothing
mattered but the two of them. There were no responsibilities, no bills to pay, no brother to worry about.
No clock ticking away their time together.

Just Gavin's arms around her, his hip next to hers,
his mouth devouring hers as if he were starved for the
taste of her. Her own needy hunger answering his, her
fears shoved aside. No room for them here.

She dug her fingers into his shoulder and gripped
him hard, ignoring the hoots and hollers from those
standing in line for the next ride as the wheel carried
them down, down, along the ground, then started back
up. She floated with it, with him, but the sense of free-
dom came from his mouth on hers rather than from the
ride. Oh, but his mouth was magic. Soft, smooth. Gentle now. Easing away.

Her eyes fluttered open to find his watching her with
a question, and a hint of wariness, in their deep blue
depths. In answer, she smiled. "You taste like cotton
candy."

Relief flashed through his eyes, as though he'd been

afraid she would object to his kiss. After the way she'd acted yesterday, she couldn't blame him.

But tonight she wasn't Anna Collins, dull, dependable bookkeeper. Tonight she was...Cinderella. He was her own personal Prince Charming, and she was having a ball.

She refused to let herself think about what would happen when the clock struck midnight.

When they left the Ferris wheel, Gavin took her hand and headed up the street. "Come on. Let's find that photographer and have that old-timey photograph done."

She had to rush to match his long-legged stride. "Is it one of those places where we stick our heads through holes in giant pictures?"

"Uh-uh. This one's got costumes."

She batted her eyes at him. "I don't think I want to be a schoolmarm. I'll be the dance hall queen and you can be the dashing gambler."

Without missing a stride, he gave her a quick kiss. "We can be anything you want."

She laughed. "Actually I don't think I have the nerve."

"Sure you do."

"We'll see." But just then one of the stands at the corner caught her eye. It only took her a second to decide. If she wasn't herself tonight, and if she really could be anything she wanted... "Stop."

Gavin whipped his head around to find out why she was suddenly tugging him in the opposite direction. "What?"

She looked at him with pure devilment in her eyes. To see her this way, laughing and outgoing as she'd been all night... This, Gavin knew, was the real Anna, the one she kept buried because she'd built her entire life around duty and obligations and a brother who drained her spirit. Tonight she was so animated, so alive and vibrant, she took his breath away.

"You think we should?" she asked, motioning toward the stand in front of them.

Gavin's grin came fast and spread wide. "You're on your own this time. I don't go in for things like that."

"Ah, come on," she wheedled. "I won't have the nerve unless you do it, too."

His smile softened. "You've got a hell of a lot more nerve than you think."

She laughed. "I think I'm finding that out. But I still won't do it alone. Come on." She started dragging him toward the stand.

What the hell, Gavin thought, letting her pull him along. What was one little tattoo, anyway?

In the rearview mirror, the bright lights of Reno grew smaller as the Corvette flew east into the night. Next stop, Oklahoma.

Stayed a little too long in Reno, Ben admitted silently. Just like he'd done in San Francisco.

Sorry, Anna, he thought, chagrined. *I wasn't going to come to you, but now I don't have a choice.* He'd stepped in it good and proper this time. He was up to his eyeballs, and that was a fact. Yesterday he had heard that Gavin was looking for him. It was going to be bad enough facing him after taking his car. Ben could admit now that that had been a damn stupid thing to do.

But he couldn't go back without also paying off what he owed Gav. He had to have that money in hand. For once in his life he had found something more important than gambling and good times—Gavin's friend-ship.

And my latest stunt may have ruined it all.

He had one chance now, and that was Anna. Anna would fix it. She always fixed things for him.

She was sure gonna be surprised to see him, he thought with an uneasy glance toward his passenger seat. Oh, yeah, she was gonna be surprised, all right.

But this would be the last time, he vowed, that he would go to her for help. The very last time. He hoped.

Chapter Eleven

Anna and Gavin got matching tattoos, but she chickened out on the dance hall costume.

By the time they left the park it was after ten and Anna was pleasantly exhausted. The ride home on the bike, even though it was still eighty degrees, was chilly. She used it as an excuse to snuggle up against Gavin's back.

When they reached her driveway she climbed off the Harley and raised the garage door for Gavin to pull in beside her car. The heat of the day still lingered there, warming her cool skin. Before Gavin turned off the headlight she turned on the overhead light and waited for him at the kitchen door.

There was something, as Gavin approached her, something warm in his eyes. "Thank you," he told her quietly.

Her breath sighed out. "For what?"

"For tonight. I've never enjoyed a night this much."

Anna shook her head. "I should be saying that to you. It was the most special night of my life," she whispered. She touched his cheek with her fingertips, surprised at the way his eyes slid shut and his face turned in to her hand. It seemed to her that there was a sudden lack of air in the garage. Either that, or her lungs had forgotten how to work.

He cupped his hand over hers and pressed a kiss to her palm. Such a simple gesture, such a complicated response inside her. Hot tingles raced from the spot where his lips touched her, straight down to the pit of her stomach, and lower. Emotions swelled. Needs rose.

He threaded his fingers through hers, brought their hands down together, and opened his eyes. "Let's go inside, Anna."

What his words asked might have been simple, ordinary. But his eyes asked for a different kind of entry. With her gaze trapped by his, she opened the door at her back and stepped into the house.

She'd left the light on over the sink. It gave an intimate glow to the kitchen as they crossed the floor. In the living room she turned on the lamp, disappointed when Gavin released her hand to move toward the stereo. A moment later, soft, soulful music filled the room.

Gavin held out his hand. "Dance with me," he said in that hushed, husky voice.

Anna hesitated, suddenly self-conscious. "I'm not very good."

"I don't care." And he didn't. But he didn't think she'd say yes if he just came right out and asked to hold her. He wished she hadn't reminded him last night that he'd be leaving soon. He couldn't get it out of his head. He didn't want to waste any more time. He wanted his arms around her, hers around him. He kept his hand extended, and waited what felt like an eternity.

Finally she reached out and touched her fingers to his. It took an incredible amount of control to keep from grasping her and dragging her into his arms. He took a slow, deep breath and let it out, letting the music ease him.

When she stepped near, he took her hands and slid them around his neck, slipped his around her waist. Gently he pulled her close. He swayed to the slow beat of the music, and Anna followed him easily enough, though he felt the tension in her muscles.

"Whose music are we listening to?" she asked, arching back to look up at him.

"That's Boyz II Men." He slid a hand up to cup the back of her head and press her cheek against his shoulder. "Their newest 'Babyface' CD."

"'Babyface'?" Anna asked, to keep him talking. She loved the way his voice rumbled in his chest beneath her ear, comforting, hypnotic. Soothing. Arousing.

"Another artist. He wrote the songs, sings with them on this CD."

She nuzzled her nose against him. "It's nice. I like it. When do I get to hear some of your songs?"

Gavin hadn't realized he'd wanted her to ask. With most women, when they asked about his music, he cringed, because the next question was, invariably, how many famous people did he know. With Anna, a warmth spread through his chest. "Do you want to?"

She raised her head and looked up at him. "What a question. Of course I do."

"We'll go pick some up tomorrow, if you want."

"Why do we need to buy them? You brought a guitar with you. Why haven't I heard you play it?"

Gavin shook his head. "I don't sing. Don't have the voice for it."

Anna frowned. "I don't believe that. I like your voice."

His lips twitched. "Maybe that's because you haven't heard me sing."

"Will I ever?"

"Hear me sing?"

"Yes." She gazed up at him, her heart racing. "We're running out of time, aren't we."

He lowered his forehead to hers. "Not tonight." He pressed his lips to her temple. "Tonight we have all the time in the world, and I want to spend it holding you."

The music swirled around them, soft, evocative, voices blended in perfect harmony singing of love, of loss, of heartache.

Gavin ran his hands down her back, pulling her closer. "You feel so damn good."

His words made Anna's heart swell in her chest. An empty, aching void opened up low inside of her. She turned her face into his neck and tasting him seemed the most natural act in the world. He tasted warm, slightly salty. Exotic. That her simple gesture should make him shudder was more heady than any wine. It filled her with confidence, with power. With the desire for more.

"Please," he whispered, "do that again."

She did it again, and felt his body's unmistakable response as he hardened against her abdomen. This time it was Anna who shuddered. When he cupped her hips and pulled her closer, pressed her softness tight against his hardness, a bubble of heat and moisture burst down low inside her. She thought her knees might buckle.

He whispered her name and rained kisses down the side of her face until he worked his way to her lips, leaving a trail of fire in his wake, soft fire, beautiful fire that turned her muscles to putty. Under the pressure of his mouth, her lips parted, her neck weakened.

Her response threatened Gavin's control. He couldn't let that happen. Not for his life would he send her running from him, hiding again behind distant politeness. Tonight he'd seen the real Anna, the warm, outgoing, fun-loving person she kept hidden from the world for fear of being hurt. He wondered if she had any idea how devastatingly appealing it was to him to watch her come alive the way she had tonight, the way she did with her music. He would cut off his right arm before he hurt her by pushing too hard, too fast.

Oh, but how he wanted her. Wanted her to the point of obsession. But he would settle for this, for tasting her, for tracking kisses along her jaw, raking his teeth gently down her throat until she shivered with it.

"I thought," she said with a gasp, "we were supposed to be dancing."

Against her neck, Gavin smiled and nibbled. "I forgot." He pulled the tucked-in sweater free of her jeans and spread his eager hands across the warm silky flesh of her back. "You make me forget a lot of things," he added, reminding himself that there were things, like his leaving, that he had no business forgetting. Mindful of that, he resumed the slow fluid movement of the dance, pulling her closer, savoring her. Wanting her.

The feel of his hands on her skin wiped from Anna's mind any thought of sense, of practicality, of self-preservation. Her mind filled with him, only him, and the music of love that swirled around them. "What are you doing to me?" she whispered.

"Dancing." With teeth and tongue and lips, he nibbled her earlobe. "Just dancing."

More heat, more moisture, pooling, flooding her. "And if I want more?"

He stilled. His feet, his hands, his mouth. Stilled. Until slowly he raised his head to look into her eyes. He searched, probed, as if he could see into her very mind. "Anna?"

She'd never seen a hungry wolf before, but she imagined this was what his eyes would look like. Hot, avid. Dark. "Kiss me," she whispered.

He didn't need a second invitation. His mouth swooped, captured, ravished. He made demands with his lips that she never thought to deny. She had demands of her own. His tongue slid against hers, rough velvet. When he retreated, she followed. One of them groaned. She didn't know who, didn't care.

That part of him that was pressed against her abdomen grew harder. She pressed against it with instinct as old as time, wanting closer, wanting to crawl inside his skin, become a part of him, wanting him to become a part of her.

But his mouth, oh, his mouth. She couldn't think, didn't want to. Wanted only to savor the moment, the night. She didn't know how her bra came to be unfastened, didn't care. Nor did she care that she couldn't stop the tiny whimpers of need coming from her throat when his hands slipped around to brush the sides of her breasts. *Touch me.* Oh...if he didn't touch her she would go mad. She squirmed against him, twisted into his touch until he covered her aching breasts with those hot, strong hands.

Heaven. She was floating in sheer heaven. Yet it wasn't enough, not nearly enough. Something was missing. She didn't know what until his thumbs skimmed over her nipples.

Fire shot straight to her core. She threw her head back and cried out, unable to contain the pleasure that was nearly unbearable.

At her response, the way her head rolled back, her eyes closed, her mouth open and gasping for breath, one thread of Gavin's control snapped. In an instant he whipped the sweater off over her head. He had to taste, to touch. But first, he wanted to see her.

Her skin was creamy pale, her breasts full, nipples aroused. "Beautiful," he whispered as he leaned and took one of those hard, enticing nipples into his mouth. Her cry of pleasure, the way she dug her fingers into his shoulders, urged him on, as if he'd needed urging. He craved her taste, the feel of her on his tongue, the way a drowning man craves air.

Then her hands were clawing at his T-shirt, delving beneath it to his skin. A shudder of pleasure racked him. He ached with wanting her, in his loins, in his heart. Even what few brain cells he had that were still in working order ached with wanting her. With his hands on the backs of her thighs, he lifted her until she wrapped her legs around his waist.

As he trailed his mouth from the tip of one breast to the other, he couldn't stop his hips from flexing, pressing his hardness against the very heat of her. The torture was exquisite. Holding her close, he staggered backward and settled on the edge of the couch, where he could lean back and take her weight, all of her, without removing his mouth from her breast. If he moved his mouth, he would die.

Anna became dimly aware that they were on the couch, that she was straddling him, and could only be grateful that her knees weren't expected to hold her any longer. What he was doing to her with his mouth, with the way he flexed his hips into hers…she couldn't think, didn't want to think. But she wanted to feel him. It didn't seem fair that he should still be wearing a shirt. How dare he still be wearing a shirt.

She struggled with it, tugged and pulled, but in the end he had to help her because her hands were shaking and her brain sent out conflicting signals to her fingers. Touch him. Get rid of the shirt. *Touch him.*

"Yes," Gavin whispered harshly. "Touch me. Let me touch you."

"Yes," she answered, breathless. "Yes."

She splayed her hands across his chest, marveling at the sleek hardness of muscles, thrilling in the way his hands mirrored the movements of hers. When she trailed her fingers across his nipples, he released her breast. He sucked in a sharp breath and arched against her.

"You like that," she said in wonder.

"Like?" His single laugh was harsh. "If you do it again I might embarrass myself."

Again she felt that sense of power surge through her, power that she could make this strong man gasp with just a touch. It was heady. Thrilling. She did it again.

Gavin used his own hands to still the movement of hers. His chest heaved for breath. "I think…we need to slow down."

"Is that what you want?" Mercy, was that her voice, so low, so deliberately provocative?

"What I want," he said hotly, releasing her hands and strumming his thumbs over her nipples until she cried out, "is to tear those jeans off you and bury myself so deep inside you that I never find my way out. I want to give you so much pleasure that you scream with it."

Fear sapped the strength from her shoulders and skimmed down her spine—of course it was fear, it had to be fear. He wanted to make her scream.

Gavin felt her shiver and cursed himself. "I'm sorry. I didn't mean to scare you." He knew he should take his hands from her breasts, but he couldn't bring himself to. "I won't hurt you, I'd never hurt you, Anna." He couldn't see her eyes. She had them closed. Because she was too embarrassed? Shocked by what he'd said? "Anna?"

She raised her head slowly and looked at this man who'd come into her life and turned it upside down with his smiles, his laughter, his music. His touch. His kiss.

He wanted to make her scream. *With pleasure.*

Yes, there was fear, of the unknown. But there was desire, and need, in such quantities as she'd never known. And now he was afraid he'd scared her away. "Gavin..." she heard herself whisper as she lowered her lips to his. "Make me scream, Gavin. Make me scream with pleasure."

For one brief instant everything inside Gavin stilled. Just shut down. Heart, lungs, mind. Then his lungs leaped for air, his heart thundered. His mind just flat disappeared. She was offering him heaven, with her mouth ravaging his—had a woman ever demanded so much with her mouth before? With her thighs open to him, straddling his hips, pressing her moist heat, heat he could feel even through her jeans and his, right where he wanted it, needed it.

Make me scream with pleasure.

He might die trying, but she would scream, he vowed to himself. With pleasure. And when she screamed, it would be his name. Only his. She was his.

And he, he was coming to realize, might very possibly be only hers.

In a movement to make a contortionist jealous, Gavin wrapped one arm around her hips, the other around her back, and somehow made it from the couch to his feet without breaking the kiss. Bed. He wanted her in bed, where they could stretch out and enjoy each other. He took a step in that direction, then cursed sharply.

With his mouth suddenly gone from hers, Anna raised her head, dazed. The room was swaying. "What…"

"Sorry," he muttered. "Just hold on to me."

"What happened?"

"Your coffee table just scored another point on me."

She hadn't expected, amid the heated passion, to experience laughter, but she felt it bubbling up inside her.

"If you laugh," he warned playfully, "I'll bite you."

Threading her fingers together behind his neck, she leaned back to see the laughter in his narrowed eyes. But there was heat there, as well, and it stole her breath. "Yeah?"

Surprise flared in his eyes at her breathless, sultry tone. "Yeah." Stepping carefully around his wood-and-glass nemesis, he kept his eyes locked with hers as he carried her across the room.

Because she still had her legs wrapped around his waist, every step he took thrust him intimately against her. Her head fell back, her eyes slid closed. "Where?"

He nuzzled her throat with lips and tongue. "Your bedroom."

A bubble of laughter broke loose. "You're going to bite me in my bedroom? What part of my anatomy is that?"

"I'll show you." He smiled against her throat. "But first I'm going to bite you in your hall." With a low growl, he raked his teeth down the side of her throat.

"Oh, I like..." Breathless with the sensations swamping her, the racing blood, the pounding heart, she arched to give him better access. "Being bitten...in my hall."

"Yeah?" When he felt the bed against his legs he sighed with relief and took her down slowly, gently.

"Yeah."

The only light was the dim rectangle of the doorway, lit from the living room lamp. In the darkness of the room, he kissed her. He could take his time now. He still ached, was still desperate, still hard, but she was here in his arms, and that staggering rush of urgency loosened its claws and made room for tenderness.

Anna nearly wept with it. She'd expected...she didn't know what. A hurried fumbling in the dark to get the deed done?

Not with Gavin. He took his time raining kisses and tenderness across her forehead, her cheeks, her nose. Down her jaw and over her lips. He kissed her neck and lapped at the hollow of her throat with the tip of his tongue.

His lips trailed over the slope of one breast, then the other. Her breasts seemed to swell to meet his mouth.

Their peaks tightened and begged for attention. Then he gave it, his mouth on one, his fingers on the other, strumming, plucking on invisible wires that reached to her core, opening a yawning, aching emptiness that cried out to be filled with him, only him.

He made as if to leave her breast. In protest Anna slid her fingers through his hair and urged him to stay.

In response he suckled harder, drawing her into his mouth. She was going to fly apart.

The needy sound that came from her throat drove Gavin wild. He forgot about tenderness, about going slow, as he pleasured himself, and her, at her breast. Her fingers clutched his head, held him there, right where he wanted to be.

But she had two breasts, and he wanted them both, had to claim them both. Trailing openmouthed kisses, he worked his way to the other one. And found it just as sweet, just as addictive as the first.

She moved restlessly beneath him, her legs cradling his hips. He knew what she needed, what she craved, but not yet, not yet. He couldn't—wouldn't—rush, despite the clamoring of his body for release.

He ran his hand down her ribs, savoring the silky smoothness of her skin. To reach his goal, he had to leave the cradle of her thighs. But it would be worth it, he promised himself. For both of them.

The denim at her waist was an insult to the senses. With a flick of his fingers, he freed the button and lowered the zipper. Beneath, he found elastic, cotton and heat to singe a man's soul when he slid down and cupped her.

With a startled cry of pleasure, Anna arched clear off the bed. She was dying. She had to be dying. No one could stand so many assaults on the senses and survive. But if this was death, she rushed to meet it.

When he took his hand away from between her legs she whimpered in protest. Then it was back, slipping beneath the elastic, beneath the cotton, to touch her flesh, to stroke, to delve, to drive her to madness. If this was where she was supposed to scream, she was doomed to disappoint them both. She needed air with which to accomplish it. All that came out was a strangled sob of pleasure.

Her response, the sound from her throat, the hot, wet heat as he delved inside her with one finger, snapped another thread of Gavin's control. Urgency, need, hunger. They clawed at him, forcing him to abandon her breast and pull his hand from her jeans. If he didn't get rid of her jeans and his, he was going to die. Just flat out die, and no help for it.

He wasn't ready to die. He was ready to erupt. His hands were shaking. His hands have never shaken before, not like this, not at a time like this.

But there had never been a time like this, not for him. He was thirty-two years old, and he'd been around the block a time or two. He'd had his share of women. This was different. Anna was different. She was important. She was...everything. She was *his*.

His hands shook harder. She had to help him get her shoes and jeans off. He managed his own hurriedly, then reached into his wallet for the condoms he had bought that afternoon. To give himself time to regain a modicum of control, he put one on then stretched out beside her, kissed her ear, traced a hand down one thigh, up the other. "I wish I'd turned on the light," he whispered. "I want to see you."

She made a sound in her throat that rang with impatience and thrilled him.

"You're so soft." And he was hard, and aching with it. Leaning over her, he took her mouth with his, suddenly starved for the taste of her, the dark sweetness he couldn't seem to get enough of.

When his hand skimmed up the inside of her thigh, closer and closer to the place that throbbed with need, Anna shivered. When he skimmed past to trace her other thigh, she made a sound of protest. Her blood rushed and heated. Tiny flames of need licked at her core.

Then he was over her, spreading her legs, making a place for himself. With everything she had, she welcomed him, but he only teased her, touching her, tracing a path from one inner thigh to the other with his fingers. "Please," she begged against his mouth. "Please."

The final thread of Gavin's control snapped, freeing him from restraint. He had enough sanity left to keep from plunging into her in one wild thrust, but just barely. She was hot and wet and ready for him. But she was small and delicate, so he took care, entered her slowly, a fraction at a time.

It nearly killed him. She was tight. So tight that for a minute he feared she'd never done this before. Sheer, blinding terror that he could hurt her held him still.

But she wasn't having it. She raised her hips and took him that next distance.

At finding no barrier, Gavin shook with relief.

Anna was too caught up in sensations to notice. He was filling her, stretching her. A part of him was literally inside her body, pushing away the emptiness, filling her with light, with solid heat, with pleasure so exquisite it bordered on pain.

When he started to withdraw, panic threatened. Then he thrust gently forward again and filled her more than before. Withdrew and filled. Again and again, consuming her, pulling her out of herself, joining them until there was no thought of two separate bodies, there was only one, and it was called *them*.

He took her places she hadn't known existed, dark, secret places, erotic places. Places of need and hunger, of mind-numbing pleasure. Higher and higher, until she feared she would simply fly off the face of the earth. Something was happening inside her. The pleasure and the pressure were too much. She couldn't...couldn't breathe, couldn't hold back the tide threatening to pull her under.

Gavin felt the tension mount in her, felt her resistance. "Let go, Anna." Sweat beaded his brow, his back. Blood and hips pumped harder, faster. "Let go. I won't let you fall."

And then it was happening. She'd been right—she flew off the face of the earth.

And he'd been right. She screamed.

At the sound of his name from her lips, Gavin let go and followed her over the edge. He was unaware that her name spilled from his lips.

It was some time before hearts slowed and breath came easily again. When he could, and wishing he could see her better than the dim light allowed, Gavin levered himself up on his forearms to relieve her of some of his weight. With a thumb, he traced her lips. "You okay?"

Her laugh was shaky and filled with shyness. "I don't know. Am I supposed to be?"

"You screamed."

She heard the smugness in his voice and bit back a grin. "I didn't want to bruise your ego."

"That was generous of you."

"I thought so. The music stopped."

"No." He brushed his lips over hers. "It's playing in my head. I think, tomorrow, I'll have to write it down." His teeth flashed in the darkness. "I thought you said you weren't very good at dancing."

Incredibly, she felt desire curl in her belly again. "I wasn't. Until you. You lead well."

That fast, with her simple words, he wanted her again. "Then follow me again." Later he would tell her that she'd just given him the missing piece of the song that had been writing itself in his head all evening. For now, he had better uses for his mouth than talking.

This time the loving was slow and sweet, though no less hot. He never left her, grew hard again while still deep inside. Incredible. She was incredible. And irresistible. He took them both up slowly, oh, so slowly, sending her over, holding himself back. Shifting, moving, kissing, whispering dark words. Then he did it again until he had her sobbing for breath. And yet again, but this time he went with her. It was as powerful, as life-altering, as before.

They slept then, wrapped together in each other's arms, and woke twice in the night to love again.

He finally got his wish of being able to see her, all of her, when the sun came up. She woke to find he'd pulled the covers aside—she couldn't even remember when they'd crawled beneath them. He was watching her.

She was startled to realize that instead of embarrassment, she felt pleasure at the way his eyes devoured her.

"You're beautiful," he whispered. "Perfect."

"I'm not." She stroked his shoulder, loving the feel of velvety skin over firm muscle. "But you make me feel that way."

"You," he said with a crooked smile that nipped at her heart, "make me feel like a randy teenager."

Like Gavin, Anna took advantage of the light to look her fill. He was, quite simply, magnificent, dark male flesh and lean muscle. "I don't see any pimples," she managed, becoming aroused again just looking at him.

Gavin laughed and rolled on top of her. "I wasn't talking about skin. Well, I was, but—I was talking about hormones."

"Yeah?" She grinned.

"Yeah." He traced a finger along her inner arm. "Speaking of skin, I like your tattoo."

Having forgotten it, she glanced down at her inner arm and let out a bark of laughter at the four-inch-long Harley-Davidson "Don't worry, it'll wear off in a few days" logo plastered there. Interesting, she thought. Anna Lee Collins, with a tattoo. "How's yours?" She grabbed his arm and turned it.

"Good thing it's temporary," he muttered good-naturedly as he inspected his identical tattoo. "I'd never be able to go home again. My mother would disown me."

"You didn't tell me you were risking a mother's love, and all for me." She batted her eyes.

"There's a lot I'd risk for you." The truth of his own words shook him. He kissed her. And he didn't stop until much, much later when juvenile hormones gave way to adult emotions and Gavin proved to them both that loving in the morning light was just as good as it had been in the darkness.

As they drifted off to sleep again afterward, one question pulled Gavin's mouth into a frown.

How was he supposed to leave this woman?

Why, in the name of all that was good, was he even considering it?

Chapter Twelve

She woke to music, the soft strumming of a guitar accompanying a gravelly, rusty voice.

Gavin.

Alone in her bed, Anna blushed fiercely, clear to her toes as she remembered.

Had that been her last night, and this morning? That wanton woman who had rolled across this bed in the throes of passion with a man who stole her breath and owned her heart? How was she supposed to face him after...

Oh, my. It wasn't possible to stay embarrassed when she remembered that she—dull, drab Anna Collins— had made Gavin Marshall cry out in pleasure nearly as often as he'd done the same to her. Breathless at the thought, she jumped from the bed and reached for her robe. She had to see him. Had to assure herself that last night had been real. Maybe as important to him as it was to her.

His music drew her to the den.

He wore nothing but jeans and was seated on the floor with his back to her, a pad and pencil by his side as he quietly strummed the chords. And he was singing.

"...Alone and oh, so cold, drifting along, with no one to hold, day after day, just growing old...until you."

Anna would forever regret whatever sound she must have made that alerted him to her presence and made him stop playing, stop singing.

He snapped his head around. "I didn't hear you."

"You were busy. I didn't mean to interrupt."

He leaned the guitar against the couch and climbed to his feet. "That's all right."

She smiled at him. "I thought you said you couldn't sing."

Gavin ducked his head, charming her. "That wasn't singing. That was gravel on sandpaper."

"It was singing. You should record your songs yourself instead of selling them to other artists."

He'd thought about it, Gavin admitted to himself. More than once. But it was one thing to hand your words off to someone else to sing. Quite another to have your own rough, craggy voice recorded for posterity. And if you were serious about it, you'd have to go the whole route, appearances, concerts...

"Nah," he told her. "That's not my thing."

"That wasn't something I've heard before," she said, motioning toward the notepad and guitar.

"Nobody has. I haven't finished it yet."

"May I hear it?"

He grinned. "Not until it's finished. I've been waiting for you to wake up.'' He reached for her and slid his arms around her, pulling her close. He kissed her, taking his time, savoring, enjoying. He regretted now that he'd gotten up and left her to wake alone. But the song had called him to his guitar, refusing to wait. Over the years, he'd learned to heed that call.

Besides, he thought ruefully, if he'd stayed in bed with her, they would have made love again, and he knew instinctively that Anna wasn't used to it. Or hadn't been, he thought smugly. He couldn't bear the thought of causing her any pain or discomfort.

But, damn, did she feel good in his arms.

He eased off, nibbling the corner of her mouth. ''Good morning,'' he said against her lips.

Anna sighed in utter contentment and allowed herself, if only for a moment, to lean against him, to wonder in the darkest recess of her heart what it would be like to wake every morning to his music and his kiss.

Don't look ahead, Anna reminded herself firmly. He was here now, hers now. She wouldn't spoil it wanting the impossible. ''Good morning,'' she whispered back.

''Don't clean house today.''

''What a thing to say.'' She chuckled as she stepped out of his arms. ''It's Saturday. I always clean house on Saturday. I can have it done by the time you're through working on your song.''

''I'm through working on my song, and the house is practically spotless. Let it go, just this once. Spend the day with me.''

The effect he had on her when he got that little-boy plea in his eyes, while his smile was all man, was interesting. She was supposed to resist that lethal combination?

''All right.''

* * *

They went out for breakfast, and the rest of Saturday morning raced by in a blur of color and laughter and intimate looks, of quick pecks and long, slow kisses. They found a craft fair set up in a parking lot, where Anna had to do some fast talking to keep Gavin from buying her a black velvet portrait of Elvis to hang above the CD player in her living room.

After lunch they went to the zoo. Anna had not been there since she was a child. She drank it in, loving it, but all the while more than aware that this might be her last day with Gavin. If not today, perhaps tomorrow.

She didn't mean to dwell on it. She had lived a lifetime in the past few days. The memories would warm her for years to come. She didn't want to think about how soon it would all be over.

But at the petting zoo, everywhere she turned she saw families. With children. Teens to toddlers to infants. It was the babies that drew her gaze again and again. Some fussing irritably, some grinning and cooing, some sleeping in their strollers or strapped to Mommy's or Daddy's chest or back.

It wasn't that Anna particularly wanted a baby. Not just any baby. But suddenly she knew she wanted Gavin's child. A son or daughter with vivid blue eyes and a smile that would take her breath away.

But there would be no babies for Anna. Not Gavin's. He'd been very careful last night and this morning to use a condom. At the time she had considered it thoughtful of him, even loving. Now, with reminders everywhere around her of what she would never have, she wished with all her heart that he had been less considerate.

"Anna?"

Her cheeks flushed with heat. Dear heavens, she hoped he couldn't read her thoughts. She gently eased the feeding bottle from the baby lamb's mouth and passed the bottle to the petting zoo attendant. Everywhere she looked, there were babies, she admitted with dismay. Even if they all did have four legs and a tail.

"Anna, is something wrong?"

"No." She pasted on a smile and looked up at Gavin. "Of course not. It's a beautiful day, we're at the zoo, and life is wonderful. What could possibly be wrong?"

Gavin studied her face, her eyes. "I don't know. You just looked...sad, I guess, for a minute."

"Not me," she claimed.

Claimed a little too forcefully for Gavin's comfort. As if she was trying to convince herself. There were shadows in her eyes. She was a damn poor liar.

"Come on." He took her by the hand and led her from the petting zoo area out into the regular zoo. "Let's find the monkeys." Monkeys always made people laugh. He wanted to see Anna smile again, wanted her to forget whatever was bothering her. He wanted her focused on him.

There it was, something he had never experienced before. Jealousy. Over something he couldn't even name. He didn't want Anna thinking of anything but him. Now wasn't that a fine how-do-you-do. He felt stupid and childish, and he didn't much like it. Trouble was, there didn't seem to be anything he could do to make himself feel differently.

Despite the lively antics of the monkeys, Anna grew quieter with each passing moment. But no matter how many times he asked, she continued to deny that anything was wrong.

"Do you have a headache?" he asked, his concern growing.

"No." There came that forced smile that was starting to set his nerves on edge. "I told you, nothing's wrong."

Just then a toddler a few feet away stumbled and fell, landing on his rear and letting out a loud wail. Anna jerked and reached out as if to pick the child up, but the child's mother was right there, scooping her son up into her arms.

Mortified that she had almost picked up another woman's child, Anna stepped back and turned away.

But not before Gavin finally saw and understood what was in her eyes. Yearning.

Denial screamed in his head. He had to be wrong. She had already told him she wasn't ready for a family. She couldn't now suddenly be wanting...

Oh, God, he thought.

"Come on." He took her by the hand again. "Let's get out of here."

He had to be wrong. It was his overactive imagination, that was all. Yet during the ten-minute walk back to the car, he noticed that every time they neared a young child, Anna's gaze would linger. Hungrily.

This was bad. Terrible. Disastrous.

He cleared his throat. "Is this something new for you, or do you always stare at every baby you see?"

Her hand jerked in his. Beneath his fingers he felt her pulse leap. Before she turned her head away he saw the color that washed through her cheeks.

His stomach clenched.

"I don't know what you're talking about."

Right there in the middle of the parking lot, Gavin pulled her to a stop and placed his hand beneath her chin, tilting her face until she looked at him.

He had known from the beginning that this woman had home and hearth and commitment written all over her. He'd known she wasn't the type of woman he should get involved with.

A baby, for God's sake. He could see it plainly in her eyes now. She wanted a baby. His baby.

A lump the size of Cleveland lodged in his throat. "What happened, Anna?" he asked gently, genuinely puzzled, fighting back the panic that threatened. "Did your biological clock suddenly decide to start ticking?"

Irritated, with herself as well as with his question, Anna jerked her head free. Despite the heat stinging her cheeks, she managed a slight glare. "Don't be ridiculous." She turned and headed toward the car still several rows away.

He caught up with her in two strides. "Don't do this, Anna. Don't shut me out."

Anna heard the plea in his voice as well as his words. She paused and turned toward him. With a hand on his chest, she looked into his blue, blue eyes and prayed she could put her own dreams aside before she ruined what little time they had left. "I would never shut you out."

He placed his hand over hers and pressed it harder against his heartbeat. "Then talk to me. Tell me what's going on in that mind of yours. You're starting to make me feel as though I've misled you."

"How could you have misled me?"

"I don't know, but the way you suddenly started staring at every baby within sight scares the tar out of me. You knew... Anna, you knew from the start that I wouldn't be staying."

The sharp reminder that he was only temporary in her life was like a knife to her heart, all the more painful for being true. He had never misled her, had never given her any reason to think he wanted more from her than these few days. "Yes," she whispered, "I knew."

Gavin felt her pain as if it were his own. It tore him up inside. "Anna, I never meant to hurt you."

"Shh. No." She pressed her fingers over his lips. "You haven't hurt me." She had hurt herself by letting herself fall in love with a man she knew would not stay. "You've given me so much joy. More than I ever dreamed was possible. If I want more, that's my problem, not yours. I will never ask for more from you than you're willing to give."

Gavin lowered his forehead to rest against hers. God, what was he supposed to do? "Don't let me hurt you, Anna. Please don't let me hurt you."

Anna slipped her arms around his neck and held him close. She was the one whose entire perception of herself had just been turned upside down by the sudden realization that she wanted this man's child and the knowledge that it could never be, yet he seemed to be hurting even more that she. How ironic. How incredibly sad. "I'm sorry," she whispered. "I didn't mean to ruin our day."

Gavin pulled back and looked down at her. "It's not ruined," he said huskily. "Come on, let's go home."

"Yes." She looked up at him with her heart in her eyes. "Let's."

It occurred to Gavin on the way home that he needed to make a stop. Of all the lousy timing. After the con-

versation they'd just had, how the hell was he supposed
to admit he was out of condoms?

Just do it, pal. You know you have to.

He did know it. No matter what she thought she
wanted, he could not take the chance of getting her
pregnant. He would not be the one to ruin her dream
of college, and he would not get married simply because he'd gotten careless with birth control.

A few blocks from her house he pulled into a drug-
store parking lot.

She looked at him expectantly.

Gavin took a deep breath, then swallowed. "Unless
you want me to sleep in Ben's bed again, or on the
couch, I need to make a purchase."

Another knife to her heart, Anna thought, and this
time it twisted even more cruelly. But she had gone
into this with her eyes open, and she wasn't willing to
end it simply because she wanted more than he offered.
She would take whatever he would give her, and be
glad of it.

"Don't buy them on my account," she told him quietly. "But no, I do not want either of us to sleep alone
tonight."

He touched a thumb to the corner of her mouth.
"You might not think so, but I am buying them on
your account. I have to, Anna. Don't make this harder
than it has to be."

She gave him a wobbly smile. "When did you get
to be so darn responsible?"

His lips curved slightly. "For a rock-and-roll songwriter, you mean?" Then his smile died. "Don't let
me be the reason you lose your dream of college.
Please don't."

Heavens, she loved this man. "Go buy your condoms, Gavin. I'll be waiting for you."

They spent the rest of the afternoon watching old movies on television. They sat close and held hands, with Anna's head resting on Gavin's shoulder, each feeling their time together slip away moment by moment.

It was barely dark that evening when Gavin gently lifted Anna in his arms and carried her to bed. "I want you."

Anna clung to him and fought the urge to tell him how much she loved him. Such an admission from her would only make him feel worse. She wouldn't do that to him. She would stick to her promise to take only what he was willing to give. When he tore open the condom wrapper a few minutes later, she knew that it was for the best.

Then he proceeded to make her forget that she had ever wanted anything but his touch. She lost herself in the moment and gave him everything she had, everything she was. And afterward, when they both returned to earth, they started the journey again, together.

"The sun's coming up," he murmured.

"I guess," she said, nibbling on his earlobe, "we didn't get much sleep."

That fast, just a nibble on his ear, and he wanted her. Fiercely. But first he had to see into her eyes. He rolled and shifted until she was sprawled atop him and straddling his hips.

"I guess," she said breathlessly, "we're not about to."

Gavin let out his breath. The shadows were gone.

She met his gaze squarely and smiled easily, fully. Naturally.

He smiled back and brushed a thumb over her nipple, gratified by her sharp intake of breath. "I was hoping you'd say that." She was the most generous, giving lover he'd ever known.

Anna kissed him, feasting on his lips. When he ran a hand down her spine and cupped the heat of her, her hands fisted in his hair. She felt his clever fingers stroke and probe, and her mind blanked. There was only him, only his mouth, his touch. She could barely hear the sound of harsh breathing over the thundering of her own heartbeat in her ears. Gasping for breath, she tore her mouth free.

Gavin took instant advantage, pulling her up until the tip of her breast filled his mouth. Her cry of pleasure urged him to suck harder. She was so sweet, so responsive. And she was driving him out of his mind.

With his hands at her waist, he lifted her until she rose above him, poised where he needed her, where he knew she needed him. "Take me, Anna. Take me."

Slowly, one exquisite inch at a time, she sank onto him, taking him deep inside, all the way, to the hilt. He nearly shouted at the glory of it, of feeling her surround him, seeing her above him, her wide gray eyes hot and smoky. She pulled his hands up her ribs until he cupped her breasts. Keeping her hands over his, she began to move, slowly, surely, wringing one moan after another from him as her eyes slid shut and—

"What the hell is going on here?"

The bubble of intimacy and passion they'd stolen for themselves burst, shattered by the voice of Ben Collins from Anna's open bedroom door.

Gavin's gut clenched. Anna's eyes went blank with shock. Gavin swore viciously and grabbed for the sheet, trying to shield her from her brother's condemning eyes.

Anna stared at her brother, paralyzed with horror.

"Anna," Ben cried. "For God's sake!"

With a sharp cry, she folded in on herself and fell against Gavin's chest. "Get out," she gasped, hunching her shoulders in mortification. "Get out!"

Gavin wrapped her in the sheet and held her tight. "You heard her," he snarled. "Get out."

"You get out," Ben shouted. "Get out of my sister's bed, you son of a bitch."

"Ben," Anna cried, her voice muffled against Gavin's neck. "Just get out. Get out of my bedroom!"

"I'm not leaving you here alone with him."

Gavin's temper exploded. "You wanna take me on, you little weasel?" He rolled Anna to his side, jumped from the bed and stepped into his jeans.

"Gavin, no," Anna cried.

"What gives you the right," Gavin demanded through gritted teeth, ignoring her and advancing on Ben, "to walk into your sister's bedroom uninvited, unannounced?" He grabbed Ben by the collar and dragged him from the room.

Shivering in reaction, Anna allowed herself a full five seconds to huddle beneath the sheet. Then humiliation gave way to rage. How dare her brother walk in that way and pass judgment on her and Gavin? How *dare* he?

And how dare Gavin...

How dare Gavin what? Defend her honor?

Tears stung her eyes. Adding herself to the list of people she was angry with, she dashed the tears away and grabbed her robe, intent on putting a stop to the shouting in the living room before things got out of hand.

When she reached the living room a few seconds later she realized things were already out of hand. Gavin and Ben stood nose to nose, Gavin's eyes narrowed to furious slits, his fists clenched at his sides.

Ben's face was beet red. "I won't have you amusing yourself at my sister's expense, damn you."

"Amusing myself?" She'd never heard Gavin's voice that quiet, that steely. "Is that—"

"Stop it! Both of you, just stop it right now."

Both men, chests heaving, kept one eye on each other when they turned to her.

"I can't believe," Ben said to her, "that someone with as much common sense as you've got would fall for whatever line this bastard used."

"You're digging a hole, kid," Gavin said coldly. "And I'm gonna bury you in it."

"Anna, can't you see he's using you? What better way to get to me than to cozy up with my sister?"

"I think you've said enough," she told him.

"Think about it, Anna," Ben said desperately. "Why else would a rich, famous songwriter come on to a woman like you?"

Anna reeled as though he'd slapped her. The blood drained from her head. Her stomach rolled. "A woman like me?"

"Way to go, jackass," Gavin snarled. "How many more ways can your pea-size brain come up with to insult her?"

"I'm not insulting her. Anna knows what she is. She's *nice*, and she's good, and she's nothing like the party girls you hang out with." To Anna he said, "He's

only here because I owe him money. You pay him off
and watch how fast he leaves. It's not you he wants,
it's his lousy five thousand dollars.''

It hurt. Oh, God, it hurt. The truth of her brother's
words sliced to the bone.

Gavin gripped her arm. ''Anna, don't—''

''It's all right, Gavin. We both know he's right.''

''He's not right, and you know it. Things changed.
You know they did.''

''Pay him, Anna,'' Ben urged. ''Pay him off and get
rid of him.''

''She gonna pay me, too?''

Anna whirled toward a new voice from the couch.
Stunned, she could only stare. The man rose slowly to
over six feet. He had to weigh at least two twenty-five.
His head was as bald as a baby's behind and he wore
a wide gold hoop in one ear. When he crossed his beefy
arms over his chest, he looked, incredibly, like Mr.
Clean. But Mr. Clean had never leered at her that way,
making her feel dirty and exposed.

A shudder of revulsion tore through her. ''Who are
you?''

''I'm Rocko.'' He grinned, showing a shiny gold
front tooth. ''Rocko Mariano from Reno. Your little
brother said you'd pay his debt, but he forgot to mention what a looker you are. If you don't have enough
money, maybe we can work out a trade, you and me.''

Gavin snarled and started forward, but Anna blocked
him with her arm. Horrified, she kept Gavin at bay and
whirled on Ben. ''You dare?'' she whispered harshly.
''You dare bring one of the goons you owe money to
into my home?''

''I didn't have any choice,'' Ben said tightly. ''If

you'll just lend me a little, I can pay him off and he'll leave."

"Anna." Gavin's fingers dug into her arm. "Don't do it."

"How much?" she snapped to Ben.

For the first time, Ben looked uncomfortable.

"How much did you lose this time?" Anna demanded.

"Not much. Just six. Grand."

Anna's heart stopped. "Six...thousand? Dollars?"

Gavin let go of her arm and turned on Ben. "You stupid, self-centered bastard. She's not buying your way out of this mess. Not this time, you little weasel."

Ben's gaze had lowered, but suddenly his eyes bulged as he stared at Anna's arm. "Good God, a tattoo?" He snarled at Gavin. "What the hell have you done to my sister?"

"Ben—" Anna began.

"Dammit, Anna." Gavin whirled on her.

"Pay him and get him out of here, Anna," Ben urged. "Get him out of here before he ruins you completely."

"You're not giving up your college again for this ungrateful jerk."

"Come on, Anna," Ben wheedled. "You know you've always got a little extra tucked away."

"Six thousand dollars?" she said again. "Plus the five you owe Gavin?" She looked at Ben as though she'd never seen him before.

"Whatever money she's got is what she's saved up for her college," Gavin said with a snarl.

"Get off it, Marshall. Anna's never been to college."

"And why do you think that is?" Gavin mocked.

"Could it be because every time she saves up enough money, you come dragging in here with some sob story? You're pathetic, Collins. A mooching little weasel who'd rather live off his sister, no matter what it costs her, than stand on his own two feet and act like a man for a change."

"So much for friendship," Ben muttered.

"Friendship?" Gavin glared. "Yeah, I thought we were friends. Until I made the same mistake she makes by believing you when you said you'd pay me back. You paid me back, all right. Took my money, took my car, and took off. So help me, if you've put so much as a ding in the door, I'll rearrange your face."

"That's enough," Anna said quietly. "Gavin's right about one thing, Ben. I am going to college. I start this fall. That means I don't have any money to give you."

"Come on, Anna, I'll pay you back by fall, I swear it."

She saw the panic in his eyes, heard the desperation in his voice. Saw the way the thug across the room narrowed his eyes into menacing slits.

"No," she told him, her insides freezing into a hard knot. "I'm through being used. By anyone." She met Gavin's eyes and held them.

Gavin felt a sliver of panic prick him. "Anna—"

"I'm going to go take a shower now." She felt dazed. Battered and bruised. "When I come out, I want all of you gone."

Ben protested viciously.

Gavin held her gaze. "I'm not leaving, Anna."

"Why not?" She smiled at him sadly. "It was fun while it lasted, but you came to get your hands on my brother. Well, here he is. You can take him and go home now. Like I said, I'm through being used. By anyone."

"Anna, don't do this. I love you."

Anna heard him, but the words barely registered. They were too far-fetched to be believed. Gavin didn't love her. He had made that more than plain yesterday.

Too much of what Ben had said echoed her own fears. She was just dull little Anna Collins. Had it been only two days since she'd reminded herself that a man like Gavin could never be serious about a little mouse like her? How right she had been.

Oh, she didn't doubt that he cared. A little, at least. But love? No. He was only trying to make her feel better.

"That was sex, Gavin, not love. Really good sex, but it's over now. You've got what you came for. You can go home." She turned her back and walked away.

Ben snickered. "Guess she told you."

Gavin didn't say a word. He just turned to Ben and punched him in the mouth. Seeing the son of a bitch stretched out on the floor did wonders for the black mood engulfing him at Anna's stinging rejection. Gavin had never told a woman he loved her before. Anna was a first for him. She was in his blood, and she'd just ripped his heart to shreds without batting an eye.

As he grabbed Ben's collar and pulled him from the floor, he was feeling particularly ugly. "Are you satisfied now, you worthless piece of—"

"Hey, all I did was tell her the truth."

"The truth?" Gavin demanded, incredulous, furious. "Is that how you see your sister? As some perpetual old maid no man would ever be attracted to?"

Ben gaped, stunned. "I never said anything like that."

"It was close enough, and that's what she heard. You just sliced your sister to ribbons. You're not fit to even speak her name."

The stranger by the couch took a step toward them. "You wanna save the family spat for later? I want my money, Collins. You said you'd get it here."

Looking decidedly uneasy, Ben ran stiff fingers through his hair. "You'll get it, man. I just need to talk to my sister again. As soon as she gets out of the shower—"

"You won't be here when she gets out of the shower," Gavin told him coldly.

"Neither will you." Ben glared. "She told you to get out, too."

"You can both get out," the man said, grinning like a crazed jack-o'-lantern. "I'll make my own deal with Sis."

Gavin's blood ran cold. "You brought this creep into her home? Were you out of your *mind?*"

"Yeah, well." Panic seeped into Ben's eyes. "It would have worked out fine if you hadn't been here, putting ideas in her head."

"What kind of ideas? That she's entitled to a life of her own? That she shouldn't have had to dream and scrimp and save for *twelve years* for enough money to go to college because you kept bleeding her dry every time she turned around? That her brother is a grown man and she's not responsible for his stupidity? Or maybe you mean the idea that she's a beautiful, desirable woman that any man would be proud to call his. What's the matter, Ben? Can't stand to realize that somebody or something else other than you might be important to her? Grow up, damn you, and grow up fast, before you completely destroy her."

Rocko from Reno propped hands the size of whole hams on his linebacker hips. "Ah, hell, man, you're breaking my heart. Is somebody gonna pay me my six grand plus expenses, or do I need to take it out in trade from Sis in the shower?"

Ben gulped. "Expenses?"

"Hey, I rode in with you. I got no way home, man. You owe me for that."

Ben's smile was shaky and full of nerves. "Okay, okay. As soon as she comes out—"

"No way in hell," Gavin said. He was afraid that Anna would give in and pay the bastard, just to get rid of him. Gavin wasn't about to let that happen. He wasn't about to let Ben or the bruiser with the earring stay under her roof one more minute. He jabbed a finger toward the guy's chest. "Stay."

He swore all the way to his bedroom. The room he hadn't slept in for two nights. He was going to have to leave her, leave with everything unsettled, with her not believing he loved her. All because of that overgrown juvenile delinquent of a brother of hers. Gavin knew Ben wouldn't leave unless he did. And if Gavin didn't drag him all the way back to California, Ben would just turn around and come back to Anna's.

He wasn't having it. He wasn't going to let Ben hang around and spew any more of his poison at Anna.

He dug six thousand in cash from the money belt in his duffel bag, and while he was there he finished dressing and packed all of his belongings. Seething with fury, frustration and pain, he went back out and paid the goon off. "Count it."

"Hey," Ben said, his eyes widening, his throat

working on a swallow. "Hey, man, I mean, wow, thanks, Gav."

"That's six thousand, all right. Now where's my traveling home money?"

"Oh, we'll see you get home, Ben and me. Won't we, Ben?"

"We will?"

"We will. You're going to drive him, in my car, to the airport. Just to make sure our good friend Rocko doesn't change his mind and come back here, we're going to wait with him at the airport until his plane leaves."

"Long as you buy my ticket, you don't need to stay. I've got what I came for."

"We'll wait until your plane leaves," Gavin repeated. "The two of you are going to the airport in the car and I'm going to follow on the Harley. When we leave the airport I'm going to follow you." He got in Ben's face to make his point. "All the way to my house. And if you even think about trying to lose me anywhere along the way, I'm reporting the car stolen and your ass is going to jail. You got that?"

Ben stuffed his hands into the front pockets of his jeans and swallowed. He couldn't meet Gavin's eyes. "Yeah. Sure. I got it, Gav. No problem."

Chapter Thirteen

For Anna, each day dragged out longer than the one before. At the office, Donna didn't need to be told that things hadn't worked out for Anna's "friend." She offered a shoulder to cry on, or a girl's night out, complete with serious drinking at the nearest male strip joint, whichever Anna preferred. Both if she wanted.

Anna thought—hoped—she had smiled at all the appropriate places as she turned down the offers, but she wasn't sure if she pulled it off.

She didn't seem to be pulling much of anything off lately, except sitting and staring at the wall in her living room, hugging her stupid stuffed monkey from Frontier City and picturing a black velvet portrait of Elvis while listening to the CDs Gavin had bought on the stereo he'd left behind.

She couldn't even cry. Tears meant emotion, and she had none. She was...empty. Just...empty.

Life after Gavin might have been bearable if he'd done something simple like kiss her goodbye and walk out. Instead, he'd told her he loved her.

He couldn't know, of course, how badly her heart had wanted—needed—it to be true.

But of course it wasn't true. He hadn't meant it. Maybe he had just been being kind. Maybe he'd thought he meant it at the moment, but if she had accepted his words at face value...

No, he hadn't meant it. A man like Gavin Marshall, and dull Anna Collins the bookkeeper? The idea was laughable. She had been a convenient amusement for him. Rather like his own personal Eliza Doolittle. Only instead of teaching her how to walk and speak like a lady, he'd taught her to laugh, to have fun.

She could almost hate him for that.

She had told herself as she'd huddled shivering in the shower that Sunday morning, scrubbing at that stupid tattoo until her arm was raw, that the first day would be the worst. The first day without Gavin.

She'd been wrong. Oh, it had been a nightmare, to be sure. She had felt as if she'd had ten-pound weights strapped to both arms and legs. The shock of realizing, when she had finally left the bathroom Sunday morning and found the house empty, that he left his Looney Tunes T-shirt on her bedroom floor had been bad enough. And his underwear. She'd wondered for a moment what the proper etiquette was for returning a man's Jockey's. Did one enclose a card? Say thanks for the good times?

Even more painful had been finding the photograph on her pillow, the photograph taken at Frontier City with Gavin and her dressed in costumes. The outlaw and the schoolmarm. She remembered that they'd left

the photo in the saddlebag on the Harley when they'd
come home that night. He must have found it when he
and Ben and that other man had left. Found it, and
decided he didn't want it.

All through that bleak and lonely Sunday night,
Anna told herself that this was the worst. In the morning things would start getting better.

They hadn't, of course. She had only been fooling
herself. Each day was worse, longer, lonelier, harder.
By Thursday evening, though, she thought she was doing better. At work she had managed as much as ten
minutes at a time, twice, without thinking of Gavin.

She was going to survive.

When the phone rang Thursday evening, her traitor-
ous heart leaped with hope that it was him.

"Anna?"

Her heart sank. For a moment, she couldn't speak.

"Anna, it's Ben."

For the first time in days she nearly smiled. She
could count on the fingers of one hand the number of
times he had called her over the years. As angry as she
still was with him, as hurt as she still was by the things
he'd said, he was still her brother. It was good to hear
from him. "Yes," she told him. "I believe I recognized your voice. How about me?"

A long silence, then, "What are you talking about?"

"It was a joke, Ben. Or am I not allowed to make
jokes? Is that one of the things your good ol' dependable sister just wouldn't do?"

"You know I didn't— Ah, hell, Anna, those things
I said last weekend, they came out all wrong. You
know I love you. You know I'd never hurt you on
purpose."

She sighed. "Yes, I know."

"Anyway," he said, his voice strengthening, "I was calling to let you know that I'm in California, and everything's okay. I didn't want you worrying about me."

If his calling was a surprise, his reason—just to let her know he was okay, and where he was—came as a shock. Then her heart folded in on itself. "Did Gavin make you call?"

"What, you think I can't call you on my own?"

"You rarely do, and never unless you want something."

"Well." Nervous laughter came over the line. "Guess I know what you think of me, huh?"

"Do you? Do you know that I love you very much?"

She heard him swallow. "I love you, too, Anna," he said quietly. Then, "I have a job."

Any more shocks and Anna wasn't sure she would be able to cope. "A job?"

"Well, it's not much of one. I'm a gofer at a recording studio. But it's a foot in the door, and it pays regular. And I'm playing the piano in this club three nights a week."

Gavin, she thought. Gavin had done this. "Congratulations. Two jobs. I'm impressed. What…what about the money you owe?"

"That's taken care of. I told you everything was okay."

"What do you mean, 'it's taken care of'?"

He let out a deep breath. "You're not going to believe this, but I paid them off. Everybody I owed money to."

She'd been right. She couldn't cope with another shock. "Ben…how?"

"I sold the Harley."

She managed, but barely, to pull out a kitchen chair and sit down before her knees gave.

"That's why I needed the job," Ben went on. "I sold the Harley to Gav, and he's going to let me buy it back."

"He's…trusting you to make regular payments?"

"Well…not exactly. I have to make payments for a while before I get it back. It's like it's in hock, you know? Only better, because I know he won't sell it to anybody else. I'm going to stay out of trouble, Anna. I know I've said that before, but I think maybe I've learned my lesson this time. And…you won't laugh, will you?"

She swallowed around a lump in her throat. "No, Ben, I won't laugh."

"Well, okay, it's like this. They've got this group out here that meets once a week. It's called Gamblers Anonymous. I've, uh, sorta been going, you know? Gav found 'em for me. It's good, Anna. I think I'm gonna be okay now."

Anna covered her mouth with her hand to keep him from hearing her sob.

"Anna? Say something, will ya?"

It took her a moment to compose herself. "I don't know what to say, Ben. I'm so proud of you…"

"Yeah?"

Oh, God, it wasn't enough that Gavin had bought the Harley so Ben could pay off his debts, had helped him get a job so he could buy it back. Had gotten him into Gamblers Anonymous. Now Ben was even copying Gavin's speech patterns. *Gavin, Gavin, I think you've saved him.*

"Yeah," she answered, her voice shaking. "So very proud, Ben."

"Gav's been great, you know?"

"It sounds like it."

"I'm even staying at his place."

"You're...at Gavin's?"

"Yeah, man, it's really great." He rambled on for several minutes about the huge house, the pool, the weight room.

How, Anna wondered, was she supposed to survive if every other word out of Ben's mouth was "Gavin"? He may have saved her brother, but the process was quite likely to destroy her.

Unless...

Anna sat up a little straighter as her heart started pounding. He'd said he wanted to help her brother. She'd finally come to believe him, and now she knew he was a man of his word.

I love you.

Was there a chance, however slim, that he'd meant those words, too?

Dammit, he refused to love a woman who had so little faith in him. Who did she think she was, turning her back on him when he told her he loved her? Damn her, he'd never been in love before. It was scary enough without being completely ignored.

"Okay, I did it."

At the sound of Ben's voice Gavin rammed his fists into his pockets and turned away from staring at the pool lights outside the window of his den. "Good."

"Yeah. Blew her away, man." Ben's smile was forced. "Me selling the Harley, paying off my debts, getting a job, going to the meetings."

"You told her about the meetings?"

"Yeah. She..." Ben stopped and swallowed, looked away. "I think she cried. I'm glad I called her. Thanks for suggesting it."

"I shouldn't have had to suggest it," Gavin said calmly, his heart bleeding to hear that she'd cried, even knowing she'd cried from happiness over Ben's progress. The thought of her tears nearly crippled him. "You have to start thinking, pal. Adults have responsibilities, not just for themselves, but to other people. You break her heart when the only time she hears from you is when you need money. You owe her better than that."

Ben had the good grace to hang his head. "I know." He dug gouges in the deep pile of the carpet with the toe of his running shoe. "I, uh, apologized to her for what I said to her last Sunday."

"You owed her that, too. Next time, think before you open your mouth."

"Yeah, well, I'm trying. Guess I owe you an apology, too, for what I said about the two of you."

"Meaning?"

Ben shrugged. "I guess I know you wouldn't use her like I said."

"You should." A half smile curved his lips. "But then, a guy always gets a little testy when the lady in question is his sister."

"I'm right, aren't I?"

"About what?"

"You wouldn't...you know, use her?"

"You're right. I wouldn't. Not that she believes that."

"Then I guess..."

"Guess what?"

"I guess you meant what you said to her that day, that you love her."

"I've never meant anything more in my life." He let out a harsh laugh. "For all the good it does me."

"What are you gonna do about it?"

It was a good question. It was hard to get around the pain of being kicked in the heart. Should he try again to convince her he loved her, and hope like hell she loved him back?

"Gav?"

"I'm thinking."

If emotions were numbers, Anna would know exactly what to do with them. She could pop them into a spreadsheet and make order out of chaos.

Last week she'd been empty, too numb to feel anything. This week she felt everything, and it was killing her. Joy for what had been, pain for the way it had ended. Hope that maybe if she begged, he would come back. Despair in not believing he could really love her. Horror when she remembered that the one and only time a man had said he loved her, she had turned her back and walked away.

"Your insecurities are pitiful," she told herself.

Pitiful, true, but nonetheless real.

And even if he had meant it at the time, what did she know about making a man happy, keeping him happy?

Ah, there was something she could assign a number to—zero. She knew nothing about keeping a man happy. He would surely have grown tired of her before long.

She resented her unhappiness, resented the destruction of her peace of mind. Her life had been fine before

Gavin Marshall had barged his way into it. She didn't need kites or roller coasters or fake tattoos. She had her home, her job, and she was starting college in a matter of weeks. Those things should be more than enough to satisfy her.

She hated that they weren't.

She hated even more the way anticipation tightened her stomach when the phone rang Friday evening at six.

It's Ben, she told herself. It had been just over a week since he'd called. He was probably calling—at Gavin's insistence—to tell her he still had his job, was still—please God—still going to the G.A. meetings.

"Hey, sis. I wasn't sure you'd be home."

Where else would I be?

"I mean, it being Friday night and all. I was afraid maybe you'd gone out or something."

"How are you?" she asked, ignoring his comment.

"I'm fine. Listen, I can't talk. I just called to tell you to be sure and watch 'The Tonight Show' tonight."

"Why?"

"Just do it. Promise me, Anna. You have to watch it tonight."

"Well, if it's important."

"It's life or death. Gotta run. 'Bye."

As the dial tone buzzed in her ear, Anna frowned. What in the world was that about? Was…was Ben appearing on "The Tonight Show"? He had that new job playing at a club. A job she assumed Gavin had helped him get. Ben was talented on the piano, much more so than she.

Excitement, the first she'd felt in weeks, hummed in her blood. *Oh, Ben, I'm so proud of you.*

Since she wasn't going to be able to sit still for four and a half hours until the program aired, she made herself take her time over supper, then she weeded the flower beds and mowed the yard, bagging the clippings this time just because it would take longer.

Only nine o'clock. Too much time to go. She took a long soak in the tub, adding bubbles to keep her good mood from slipping. It was wonderful to feel something positive for a change, and she didn't want to lose it.

After her bath she shampooed her hair and blew it dry.

Then she ruined it all by slipping on Gavin's Looney Tunes T-shirt. She hadn't even thought about it, just pulled it on over her head, as she'd been doing every night since he'd left.

"I'm not wearing it because it's his," she told her reflection in the mirror. "I'm wearing it because it's comfortable."

Oh, she'd learned to lie to that face in the mirror quite well lately.

She settled on the couch and watched the news, then chewed her knuckles through what felt like an hour-long sportscast. Why did they think everyone cared about sports so much that they wanted to see it for a full third of every single newscast? She ought to write a letter in protest. Why not ten minutes a night about music? Books? Local events?

Why not just start "The Tonight Show" ten minutes early, you jerks?

Then ten-thirty came.

Finally, finally, Jay Leno filled the screen with his big chin and opening jokes. Despite her tension, Anna managed to chuckle at a few of the more clever ones.

Just when she feared the monologue would go on forever, her phone rang.

No one ever called her this late at night. In fact, no one ever called her at all, except Ben.

"Anna?"

"Ben? What's all that noise?" It sounded as though there was a wild party going on around him. She heard the dull roar of dozens of voices, laughter, music. Ice tinkling in glass.

"What?" he yelled into the phone, laughter in his voice. Oh, it was good to hear him laugh. "You'll have to talk louder. We're having a little party here. Are you watching the show?"

"I was."

"What? I can barely hear you."

"I said I was," she shouted into the phone. "Until you called. Am I going to see you on my TV?"

Ben laughed. "I'll never tell. Just wanted to make sure you're watching. It's for you, Anna."

"What do you mean, it's for me? What's for me?"

"You're the reason what's about to happen on the show is about to happen. It's history-making. Just be sure and watch. Gotta go. Love you." He hung up without letting her ask what he was talking about.

Anna hung up the phone and dashed back to the living room, only to find they were in a commercial break. She was certain that there were people watching who actually cared about whiter teeth, allergy relief and new cars, but just then she wasn't one of them.

"Just get on with it," she muttered.

Finally, Jay was back. "Okay, folks, our first guest tonight is an old friend of mine I've been trying to get on the show for years."

Well, that wasn't Ben. But then he probably wasn't

the first guest of the night anyway, being brand-new in the entertainment industry.

"We finally cornered him, and he's making not only his 'Tonight Show' debut, but also his singing debut."

Singing? Ben sings? Oh, yeah…this was Jay's old friend, not Ben.

"Ladies and gentlemen, please give a big 'Tonight Show' welcome to the sensational Grammy Award-winning rock-and-roll songwriter Gavin Marshall."

"Oh." Anna pressed both hands to her mouth. "Oh, God."

On the small screen across the room, a curtain parted and Gavin walked out on stage.

In a flash Anna was off the couch and kneeling in front of the television like a supplicant before an altar, her hands raised, touching the screen, wishing with all her heart that it was his warm, strong face beneath her fingers rather than cold, impersonal glass.

As he sat on a tall stool and picked up a guitar that had been waiting for him, Anna's chest tightened, the backs of her eyes burned. His name was a sigh on her lips.

He looked straight into the camera and said, "This is for you, Anna."

Then he began to play. And sing.

"I was alone and oh, so cold, drifting along with no one to hold, day after day, just growing old. Until you."

Anna's heart cracked wide-open. But instead of emptying, it filled to overflowing with pride—he was singing his own song instead of letting someone else sing it. The song he was writing the morning after they first made love. His husky voice, a voice she'd never thought to hear again, sent shivers down her spine and caused an ache in her chest. The courage this must be taking for a man who thought so little of his own voice.

"I never trusted love, never thought I needed it, until you."

And her heart overflowed with love, because he was singing to her. Just to her.

"I played the game, but it was all the same, until you. The road was long, with never a dawn. Until you."

His eyes. Oh, his eyes. They seemed to be looking straight into her soul.

"You turned the sky so clear and bright. In my arms, you felt so right, and the stars lit up the night, and my heart and soul took flight. I love you."

Long before the applause faded and the commercial came on, Anna knew just how big a fool she'd been the day she turned her back on him in this very room and walked away. For he did love her. She knew that now.

Ben's words that terrible day had played on every insecurity she'd ever had regarding Gavin, and what had she done? She'd opted for the safety of the familiar loneliness instead of accepting what Gavin had offered her with his heart in his eyes. She had walked away, her actions flinging his love back in his face as if it were worthless.

While a man in a furniture store claimed to be "the working man's friend," Anna wondered frantically how soon she could book a flight to Los Angeles, how she would find him—she didn't even have— His mother! She would call his mother and get his address.

But would he still want her? Could he ever forgive her for what she'd done?

Had he been saying he loved her with that song?

Or had the song been his way of saying a final good-bye?

The thought was more than her heart could bear. On her knees in front of the television, she doubled over in pain and wept.

She didn't hear the front door open behind her, didn't hear the soft oath from a heart as torn as hers. But when strong arms slipped around her, she knew. Somehow she knew that a miracle had occurred and he was there.

"Anna."

At his husky whisper, she whirled on her knees and threw herself into his embrace. "Gavin, Gavin, I love you. I love you so much. You have to forgive me, because I don't think I can go on without you in my life."

Gavin pulled away to look at her. He cupped her face in his shaking hands and wiped her tears away with his thumbs. "Shh, shh, there's nothing to forgive."

"Oh, but I was so horrible to you that day. So stupid and insecure and... Oh, Gavin, I do love you."

"Do you know now that I meant it? That I love you?"

"*Yes*. I swear I'll never doubt you again. I swear it."

"I guess you'll just have to prove it by marrying me."

Anna tried to breathe, but the instructions from her brain to her lungs must have gotten lost somewhere along the way. "Marry?" Her world reeled. A few moments ago everything had seemed so hopeless. Now he was handing her heaven. "You want to marry me?"

He brushed his lips across hers. "Say yes, Anna.

You've got on my shirt. When a woman steals a man's favorite T-shirt, she really doesn't have any choice but to say yes.''

With a cry that was half laugh, half sob, Anna flung her arms around Gavin's neck. "Yes." She kissed his ear, his cheek, his jaw. "Yes, yes, yes."

"Thank God." Gavin captured her mouth, cementing their promises to each other, vowing silently to spend the rest of his life loving this woman, making sure that love and laughter filled her days, giving her the babies she wanted, if she still wanted them. He kissed her until he was breathless. Then he kissed her again. He didn't stop until his favorite T-shirt was once again forgotten on the floor. It was another hour before they made it to the bedroom.

Epilogue

The classic, red, 1957 Corvette, with the top down, rumbled up to the curb and growled like a sleek jungle cat.

Smiling, Anna picked up her books from beside her on the grass and left the shade of the Business Sciences building for the bright California sunshine. It still tickled her to be able to wear short sleeves and enjoy the sunshine in the middle of February.

"Hey, fella." She leaned over the passenger door of the Vette. "Give a girl a ride?"

"Well, I don't know." He looked her up and down, then smiled slowly. "My wife's kinda on the possessive side."

"Is she, now? And how do you feel about that?"

"Get in this car," he said with a throaty growl that put the sound the car was making to shame, "and I'll show you."

She started to swing one leg over the door and slide into the passenger seat.

"Dammit, woman, open the door and get in the right way. You're gonna give me a coronary. Pregnant women aren't supposed to go climbing over car doors. They're supposed to be careful."

"Yes, dear."

Her meekness was nothing but a sham, and Gavin knew it, but he appreciated that she would humor him by opening the car door and climbing in like a normal person. She was only ten weeks pregnant. He knew, in the logical part of his mind, that a woman did not become an invalid just because a sperm connected with an egg and started forming a fetus.

But this was his woman, and she was carrying his baby. He was going to worry over both of them, and any other babies that might come along, every second for the rest of his life. And he was going to shower them with every bit of his love.

He had, he mused, created a monster by encouraging Anna's long-dormant sense of humor. She absolutely adored teasing him. And every time she did it, he fell that much more in love with her.

After sliding into the low seat, she closed the door sedately and turned to him, her schoolbooks on her lap. "Is that better?"

Grinning, Gavin pulled her close and gave her a long, deep kiss. "Now it is. I love you."

"I love you, too," she whispered, her eyes going soft and dark. "What do you have planned for the rest of the day?"

It had been hard for Gavin to convince her that she did not have to hold down a job while going to college after they were married, but he would be eternally grateful that she decided not to work. Even if she had insisted on paying her tuition herself. But he loved having the extra time with her in the afternoons when she wasn't studying and he wasn't working.

"Oh, I don't know," he said in answer to her question as he waited for her to fasten her seat belt. When she finished, he put the car in gear and pulled away from the curb. "I thought I'd spend the rest of the afternoon making love to my wife."

"Oh, really?"

"Yeah. Unless she's got a better idea."

"Gavin?"

"Yeah?"

She placed her hand on his knee, then slowly slid it up his thigh. "Drive faster."

"Yes, dear."

* * * * * *

Silhouette ® SPECIAL EDITION®

Newfound sisters Bliss, Tiffany and Katie
learn more about family and true love
than they *ever* expected.

A new miniseries by
LISA JACKSON

A FAMILY KIND OF GUY (SE#1191) August 1998
Bliss Cawthorne wanted nothing to do with ex-flame
Mason Lafferty, the cowboy who had destroyed her
dreams of being his bride. Could Bliss withstand his irresistible charm—the second time around?

A FAMILY KIND OF GAL (SE#1207) November 1998
How could widowed single mother Tiffany Santini be
attracted to her sexy brother-in-law, J.D.? Especially
since J.D. was hiding something that could destroy the
love she had just found in his arms....

And watch for the conclusion of this series in
early 1999 with Katie Kinkaid's story in
A FAMILY KIND OF WEDDING.

Available at your favorite retail outlet. Only from

▼ Silhouette ROMANCE™

What's a single dad to do when he needs a wife by next Thursday?

Who's a confirmed bachelor to call when he finds a baby on his doorstep?

How does a plain Jane in love with her gorgeous boss get him to notice her?

From classic love stories to romantic comedies to emotional heart tuggers, **Silhouette Romance** offers six irresistible novels every month by some of your favorite authors! Such as…beloved bestsellers **Diana Palmer, Annette Broadrick, Suzanne Carey, Elizabeth August** and **Marie Ferrarella,** to name just a few—and some sure to become favorites!

Fabulous Fathers…Bundles of Joy…Miniseries… Months of blushing brides and convenient weddings… Holiday celebrations… You'll find all this and much more in **Silhouette Romance**—always emotional, always enjoyable, always about love!

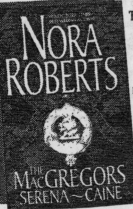

Silhouette®

SPECIAL EDITION™

COMING NEXT MONTH